OLIVER NOCTURNE

THE SUNLIGHT SLAYINGS

KEVIN EMERSON

APPLE PAPERBACKS

SCHOLASTIC INC.

NEW YORK   TORONTO   LONDON   AUCKLAND   SYDNEY
MEXICO CITY   NEW DELHI   HONG KONG   BUENOS AIRES

For J.L.B., who knows what I mean . . .

If you purchased this book without a cover, you should be aware that this book is stolen property. It was reported as "unsold and destroyed" to the publisher, and neither the author nor the publisher has received any payment for this "stripped book."

No part of this publication may be reproduced, stored in a retrieval system, or transmitted in any form or by any means, electronic, mechanical, photocopying, recording, or otherwise, without written permission of the publisher. For information regarding permission, write to Scholastic Inc., Attention: Permissions Department, 557 Broadway, New York, NY 10012.

ISBN-13: 978-0-545-05802-5
ISBN-10: 0-545-05802-3

Copyright © 2008 by Kevin Emerson
Illustrations copyright © 2008 by Scholastic Inc.
SCHOLASTIC, APPLE, and associated logos are trademarks and/or registered trademarks of Scholastic Inc.

12 11 10 9 8 7 6 5 4 3   8 9 10 11 12 13/0

Printed in the U.S.A.   40
First printing, November 2008

Contents

Prologue

The crime scene photos were grim. A boy, lying in a school gymnasium, blood around his neck . . .

"I suppose they're calling it a stabbing or something," said Detective Nick Pederson, leaning over his desk.

"The guys upstairs think it's a gang thing," Detective Sarah Laine replied.

Nick looked up at his former partner. "Really?"

Sarah nodded grimly. "Problem is, nobody can come up with a suspect, even though there were, like, ten witnesses."

Nick picked up the case report. " 'Victim died of blood loss,'" he read. " 'Happened right after choir practice . . . Witnesses described a child assailant. . . .' Well, that's gruesome."

"Tell me about it." Sarah nodded. "But . . ."

"What?" Nick peered at her. "Is there something else?"

Sarah sighed. "Here's the thing," she began, glancing over the wall of Nick's cubicle to make sure there were no curious ears nearby. Nick could have told her that she didn't need to worry. Nobody in the basement offices of the downtown Seattle police station arrived until after sundown. To say that the officers who chose desks down here worked the night shift was all too accurate. Nick was an exception: At the time that he'd chosen a basement desk, his other options had been reassignment to the traffic division or dismissal from the force.

"We found fibers on the victim," Sarah continued. "Hair. So we ran the DNA. . . ."

"And?" Nick felt his pulse picking up speed. This was like arriving at a giant lake after crawling across a desert for months.

"Well, there was a match." Sarah lowered her voice even further. "But it's not that simple: You know how we've been running DNA on our cold case archives, right?"

"This is going to be good," said Nick.

Sarah nodded. "Good if you like *weird*. The hair fibers found on this victim, they match samples from a missing person's case, but not of the kidnapper — of the kidnapping *victim*. He was taken as an infant. The hair fibers were from his stroller."

"Wow." Nick sat back. "So a kidnapped kid grew up to be a murderer —"

"But," Sarah continued, "the witnesses said a *child* did this. That kidnapping case was over sixty years ago. If this really is the same person, he'd be an old man by now, right?"

Nick didn't answer this. He gnawed on the well-chewed cap of his pen. "What about the parents of the missing kid?"

"They were killed at the scene. Christmas Eve, no less."

"So . . ." Nick scanned the photos again. "Either your DNA results are wrong or your witnesses are wrong. Or . . ." Nick eyed her. "You think there might be another answer. And that's why you brought this to me."

Sarah looked at him hopefully. "Any ideas you have, Nick . . . we're running dry upstairs, and this case is way public. It's been huge in the news. The families of the witnesses . . . they're all over us to find whatever — I mean, *who*ever did this."

Nick nodded. "I'll see what I can do. It's good to see you, Sarah."

"You, too, partner," Sarah said with her smart smile. Nick had forgotten how much he missed it. She gave him a casual salute, then walked out.

Nick sat back. His face was lit by a tiny trapezoid of February sunlight coming through the only window in the basement, right above his desk. For the past year, since Nick's demotion to the basement, he'd spent many long hours asleep in this little sliver of sun, feet up on the nearby radiator, thinking about how ironic it was that what he'd been demoted *for* had everything to do with why the other cops down here worked at night, why the one desk in the basement that got any sunlight was unoccupied, and why gruesome crimes like this Dean Aunders murder too often went unsolved in this town.

You know what did this, he thought, running his finger over the photo of red holes in a young neck. *And you know you should just leave it alone. It'll only get you into more trouble that you don't want.*

But if there was one thing Nick had learned, it was that there wasn't the trouble that you wanted and the trouble you didn't. There was only the trouble you had. And here he was, with this trouble, once again.

Nick thumbed through the case file, reading the witness testimonies: *"He looked like our age; Wearing black; There were three other older kids; Really strong; It was like they could jump really far."* He felt a rush of adrenaline he hadn't felt in too long, except . . . It was worrisome. This connection — the missing child, the young killer, the events both so close to Christmas — it wasn't much to go on, but it did beg the question: Was this *him*? Could it possibly be?

Nick picked up the phone and dialed. "Hey, it's me," he said softly. "You won't believe this, but I think I have a lead. . . . Yeah, it might be the one you've been looking for."

CHAPTER I

Old Wounds

"**W**hat's wrong with you?"

Oliver froze. He was standing over the round stone sink in the center of the bathroom, running a humming, nanodiamond stiletto file over his teeth, as he always did right before dinner. He glanced nervously across the room, to where his older brother, Bane, was drying his face with a burgundy towel.

"I — I —" Oliver stammered. What was wrong with him? How about the fact that he'd lost his friends Emalie and Dean? Or that he'd had to spend every night of this miserable last month and a half living a tangle of lies, pretending he was fine around his parents, who were lying right back to him about his future, not to mention his past?

"Relax, *lamb*." Bane scowled. "I don't mean *all* the things that are wrong with you. I mean there." He pointed at Oliver's stomach.

Oliver looked down at his thin, shirtless torso. His skin was its normal pale grayish color, and he would've known by the itching if he'd developed a mold rash, but he was shocked to find a purple wound on the left side of his abdomen, near his waist.

"Huh," said Oliver. It was a short, bright-red cut surrounded by a deep-purple oval. A small spider's web of crimson lines spread away from it.

"Looks like you got stabbed," Bane mused, "or maybe you lost a fight with a rat."

"Shut up," Oliver muttered. He hadn't even noticed the wound before, vampires being much less sensitive to pain than humans, but now that he focused on the spot, he did sense a faint, dull ache. He pulled at the skin, separating the wound. Vampires didn't bleed or get scabs, but now a bit of brown fluid dripped out. Oliver frowned at this. The fluid, the red spider lines . . . it all spelled infection. If his mother, Phlox, saw that, she'd be calling Dr. Vincent, and Oliver did not want to go back to the doctor.

During his last doctor's visit, back in December, Oliver had learned that his yearly checkups were not just to make sure he was healthy. He was also being prepared, without his knowledge, for some special but very secret purpose. Only Oliver's parents, Dr. Vincent, and perhaps some others at his father's employer, the Half-Light Consortium, knew about this plan. Last

December, all of these people had been worried about Oliver because of his sleeplessness, his anxieties, and most of all because of his *human* friends: Emalie and Dean.

Then Oliver had allegedly killed Dean, and all of that worry had turned to pride. His family had celebrated the occasion, and since then, they'd assumed he was fine and left him alone. His wasn't fine, not even close, but at least everyone wasn't worrying about him all the time. So, no doctors, thanks.

Oliver stuck his finger into the wound. He wiped away a bit of the fluid, and for a moment, glimpsed something dark red and solid-looking. Oliver dug his nail deeper —

Suddenly a searing, vampire-size pain stabbed through his body, causing his legs to buckle. Oliver toppled to the floor, smacking his head on the sink as he did so.

"Ha!" Bane spat. "Dork. Now you're probably going to go cry to Mommy and get the celebrity treatment again." Bane imitated Phlox: *"Oh, my precious Oliver, my most favorite baby! We'll drop everything to help you!"*

Oliver scrambled to a sitting position, wincing. It had been this way with Bane ever since Dean's death. Bane couldn't stand Oliver's newfound fame, which made Oliver crazy, because Dean's death was Bane's fault! After all, it was Bane who had showed up with his friends at Emalie and Dean's chorus practice — Bane who said he was there to *fix* Oliver, who made him choose a human victim to bite, and who had brought that mysterious staff. Yet Oliver didn't remember what had happened in the moments between when he'd pretended to attack Dean, in order to engineer an escape, and when he'd woken up sometime later in a classroom upstairs. According to Emalie, and Bane, Oliver had killed Dean, and there was no doubt Dean was dead, but Oliver refused to believe he'd done it, even though he hadn't been able to find any proof otherwise.

"I should drop that sink on you," Bane muttered. "That would really get Mom riled up." He gave Oliver a disgusted glance. "Enjoy the big fuss with your little injury." He stalked out.

Oliver watched him go. If someone had asked him back in December, when he was lying awake most days and wondering what was wrong with him, he would have said, for certain, that things could not have gotten any worse. Yet now, at the beginning of February, he was *still* having trouble sleeping, his brother disliked him even more, and though Dean's death had convinced his parents that he was fine, and had made the other vampire kids friendlier at school, it had also caused him to lose the only two friends he really wanted.

Oliver got to his feet and returned to the sink. He leaned back to let more light on the wound. This time he spread the skin wide, but didn't try to reach around inside, and for just a moment, he saw a flash of crimson light, like the reflection from a crystal.

It's a shard, he guessed, *from the amulet.* The amulet of Ephyra, given to him by Dead Désirée. She had claimed that the amulet was *"for his protection,"* but what it had really done was shatter, and deliver Oliver a vision of his past. In that vision he'd learned that, unlike every other vampire child, he had been *sired.* He had been a human baby and was turned into a vampire. Vampire children were normally made from the genes of their parents and grown in a special lab. A child could not be sired, because he or she wouldn't be strong enough to withstand the transformation. Yet according to that portal vision, Oliver *had* been, and his human parents had been killed by his vampire parents.

The fact that this wound in his side had been caused by the amulet was another reason why he couldn't tell Phlox about it. While it had turned out that his parents *had* secretly known about his friendship with Emalie and Dean all along, Oliver was pretty sure that they hadn't known about the amulet, nor about the vision it supplied. Oliver wanted to keep it that way until he could find out more about his past. It all felt complicated, and *complicated* was not something that vampires were supposed to have to deal with.

Oliver looked around the bathroom for something

that he could use to extract the crystal splinter. The shard didn't look that big, but it was very deep inside the wound. He considered his stiletto for a moment, but it would probably just push the shard deeper again, and that pain had been brutal. He needed long tweezers, or pliers. . . .

"Ollie!" It was Phlox, calling from upstairs. "Can you come up here?"

Oliver slipped on his T-shirt, wincing at the lingering pain. He headed back to the crypt where he and his family slept, he and Bane in their own coffins, Phlox and Sebastian in their double-wide model. He threw on sneakers and his dark gray hoodie sweatshirt.

He was halfway up the stone spiral staircase, lit by globes of molten magmalight, when he noticed a strange smell. It was something like cayenne pepper . . . and sage . . . and also *rot*. This wasn't the first time Oliver had smelled it around the house. Maybe it was some new cologne that Bane was trying out. He wrinkled his nose. Spices and decay could often smell good, but this combination didn't. As quickly as it had come over him, the smell faded, and yet, how many times in these last couple weeks had he smelled that? Hard to say. Three? Four?

Oliver entered the kitchen to find everything busy. The dishwasher was grumbling, the forge humming. His family was bustling as well — *NOT your real family!*

a voice shouted inside — and Oliver felt a familiar surge of anxiety in his gut. He took a deep breath and tried to make his face look calm and unbothered. He'd been practicing this a lot lately.

Sebastian was on the far side of the kitchen island, knotting a wide tie and stuffing it into his black suit vest. Bane was by the sink, bleaching a new streak of white into his black, shaggy hair. Phlox, wearing a shimmering silver dress and black overcoat, was carefully putting on her earrings, which were sapphires held within tiny rat skeleton claws.

"Now that we have the egg whites whipped . . ." said a smooth voice. Oliver glanced over to find Clarise Clyne, star of *Confections with Clarise*, a popular show on a human food channel, on the plasma screen over the sink. She smiled a tight-lipped smile that hid the points of her teeth as she addressed the camera: ". . . we're going to add the raspberry sauce." She produced a glass bowl of a dark crimson sauce that was steaming hot. "Of course, it doesn't have to be raspberries," she cooed at the camera with a knowing gleam in her eye. "It could be cherries, or anything else you're . . . fond of." Vampires knew what she meant.

Oliver sat on a stool at the center island. The forge timer began beeping. "Oh, good." Phlox grabbed a thick oven mitt and removed a steaming iron plate. "Here we are," she announced, sliding the dish to

Oliver. She spun quickly back to the counter, then froze. "Honey," she said to Sebastian, "have you seen the cayenne?"

Oliver perked up, watching Phlox scan the black stone countertops. "I swear it was here an hour ago," she mumbled. It was not like Phlox to lose track of anything, and this was not the first item to go missing in the last few days. Earlier in the week, Phlox had been looking for a bag of frozen Gila monster heads. Also, Sebastian had been complaining that his razor had disappeared. And worst of all, Oliver had lost something very dear and secret to him, something that he'd been keeping in one of the drawers underneath his coffin. . . .

"Haven't seen it," said Sebastian, checking his pocket watch, "but we need to go."

"Oh, well," Phlox sighed. "Sorry, Ollie, there's no cayenne." She popped open the long, sleek refrigerator mounted along the top of the wall. Its door yawned upward with a hiss, revealing orderly racks of blood bags. "What would you like to drink?" she asked. "Pig?"

"Sure," Oliver replied.

"Sorry we can't take you along, Ollie," said Sebastian, smiling warmly. "I know everyone would love to see you, and as we know, you could probably handle yourself just fine. It would also save my colleagues from hearing my bragging tales about you again."

"*Tsss,*" Bane hissed.

"Charles," Phlox warned, using Bane's real name as her hazel eyes flashed turquoise.

"But technically you're still too young," Sebastian explained, "so you'll have to wait like every other kid."

Oliver nodded, making sure he looked disappointed. Really, going to one of the Friday Socials was about the last thing he wanted to do. The Socials were large feeding events. There were a few around town each week. Everyone dressed up formally and met in the sewers. It was a big night for teens who had their demons, as well as adults. After some leisurely socializing (there were bartenders who set up stands in the sewers), the vampires would head up to the surface, to a large human gathering that had been chosen in advance, usually an all-night rave or a house party. Because the humans had been partying, they would be largely unaware. There would be some chaos, but the vampires could be fairly leisurely as they fed on the humans.

At the most elite gatherings, the humans were actually put into Staesys, freezing them in time, and then bartenders would draw the blood for the guests. Regardless of whether the humans were placed in Staesys or were simply out of it due to their own abuses, the

New World vampire code remained constant: Humans were rarely killed. They would simply wake up feeling weak the next day, and maybe a little sick, which they would think was their own doing. They might find a strange cream substance on their neck, but the bite marks beneath would already be almost gone. . . . Oliver was supposed to be looking forward to going to the Socials once he got his demon, but right now he was more than fine with staying home.

"I hope we'll find you asleep when we get back," Phlox said, kissing Oliver's head affectionately. "Maybe you'll have another dream tonight," she added hopefully, referring to the demon dreams, in which a young vampire got to know the demon that would soon come to inhabit him in adulthood. Back in December, Oliver had told everyone that he was having those dreams to hide why he was having trouble sleeping. That lie had become the truth, when during the mysterious moments leading up to Dean's death, Oliver had met his demon, Illisius, in a dream. Illisius had told him that he was destined to open the Nexia Gate and free the vampires from Earth, which some thought of as a prison. But he hadn't had another dream with Illisius since.

Sebastian ruffled Oliver's hair as he headed for the stairs. "Good morning, son."

"See ya."

Oliver listened as the heavy door to the sewers thudded shut. He dug into his dinner of Guatemalan Sepulcrit casserole (layers of brownie and fiery habanero peppers, a blood-and-cocoa mole sauce in between), then gulped down his goblet.

When he was sure that his family was gone for good, he slid off his chair and headed upstairs. He arrived at a steel door and pressed a red button. The door slid open silently. As it did, Oliver reached up into a hollow in the bare wall above the door. He felt around until his fingers found a power cord, which he pulled from a socket. This disabled the security cameras that had given Oliver away to his parents back in December. If only he'd mistrusted them before and thought to look for cameras, he might still have Emalie and Dean.

Oliver slipped around the carcass of an old human refrigerator and into the decrepit surface floor of an abandoned house. This house sat directly above the Nocturnes' underground home, concealing it from humans. He concentrated on the presence of the *forces* around him, then climbed up the wall. As he did so, he felt a dull ache in his side. He must have really aggravated that wound before. With each reach of his left arm, there was a pulse of pain. Still, he was able to move onto the ceiling and crawl to the center of the room, stopping beside a broken chandelier that hung crookedly. He flipped over and laid up against the ceiling, gazing down at the room below.

He waited and listened, but there was no sound in the dingy room except for the steady plinking of water, dripping from the ceiling into a murky bathtub in the corner. He could hear the echoes of cars through the broken windows, their tires churning in the steady rain. Now the light footwork of a rat behind one of the walls . . .

She's not coming back, stupid, Oliver scolded himself. *She hasn't yet, and she won't.* But he knew that, didn't he? *Why would she come back?* Emalie thought Oliver was a killer. *"How could you, Oliver?"* That was the last thing she'd said to him.

But she left me that article, Oliver reminded himself. The article had detailed his parents' death — *They named me Nathan* — and his abduction, long ago. *If she thought about me enough to find me that article, then maybe, when enough time goes by, she'll come back.*

But she hadn't yet.

Two weeks, Oliver reminded himself. He'd only known Emalie and Dean for two weeks. In a vampire's existence, even one only sixty-four human years long like Oliver's, two weeks was still a blink of an eye. So how could he even call them friends?

It was how she treated me, he thought. It had been so easy to be around Emalie. Things just *were*, around her.

She'd been interested, rarely disappointed, and never worried about him, as he was used to feeling from others. Oliver had sensed something sad in her, too. Her mom had left without a trace two years ago. Her dad hadn't gotten over it. Emalie had to switch schools often, as they moved from one temporary apartment to another. Despite all that, she'd radiated this hopeful feeling. It was like she woke up every day still convinced that the world was somehow this amazing place, even though it kept letting her down.

Oliver hadn't felt all this about Emalie in those brief two weeks — these thoughts had taken lots of hours, alone in this room, to put together. Really, it all just boiled down to an embarrassing thought: He missed her. *If any of them could hear that thought* . . . Oliver mused. Pick anyone from the vampire world: They would think he was hopeless.

Suddenly, a sound broke into Oliver's thoughts.

Footsteps.

From where? Oliver glanced to the refrigerator, to the window —

The door. Someone was coming. *Is she back?*

Just then, Oliver caught that overpowering scent of cayenne, sage, and rot. . . .

The door creaked open.

CHAPTER 2

A Return Visitor

A figure peered warily around the door, then stepped in. The smell was overwhelming, but beneath it, Oliver picked up some faint characteristics: It was male, and undoubtedly dead in some manner. He was tall, narrow, wearing a long coat and a black sweatshirt with the hood up over his head. He moved warily around the bottomless hole directly in front of the door, apparently not recognizing that it was really just a design trick to scare hapless humans. The actual hole was only a foot deep.

Getting past that, the figure trudged over to the bathtub. He knelt in front of it and started scrubbing at his hands. Oliver could see long, filthy fingernails, and the brown tub water wasn't helping. The figure looked at them and sighed. The sound was unmistakably sad.

He scrubbed a little more, then slapped at the water in frustration. Spinning away from the tub, he shuffled on his knees toward the wall. The figure sat down on a pile of moldy clothes, folding his long legs and then rummaging around in his coat.

Oliver crept across the ceiling to get a closer look. He recognized the smell from the staircase. What had this creature been doing in his house? Now he pulled something from his coat. Oliver saw that it was a squirrel. A meal, he guessed, but the figure just gazed down at the animal's lifeless black eyes. Oliver thought he even heard a sniffle.

More rummaging in the coat, and now there was a dull flash of metal, a familiar whiff of musk — there was Sebastian's razor. What the figure attempted to do next made Oliver wrinkle his nose with pity. He seemed to be trying to skin the animal, but a razor was no match for hide and fur. It didn't go well. After a minute, he groaned in failure and hurled the razor across the room. It skittered into the shadows.

"Gah!" he growled, and hurled the squirrel as well. He started digging around in his coat again, this time producing a bag of tennis-ball-sized objects. He pulled one out. Oliver recognized the Gila monster heads taken from their refrigerator. There was a splintering crack as the figure broke open the skull to scoop out the insides. He tossed the skull aside, stuffed the bag back in his coat, then rummaged some more. Oliver wondered what he would pull out next —

And then he saw it.

In the figure's blotchy, grimy hand was a crumpled piece of newspaper. Oliver recognized it, because it was the secret item that he had been missing: a carefully clipped newspaper article, not the one about his kidnapping that Emalie had given him. This one was more recent.

"That's mine," Oliver hissed through the gloom.

"Whu —" The figure glanced up, saw Oliver — their eyes locked, and Oliver couldn't believe what he was seeing.

"Dean!"

For a moment, Dean looked like he might run, but then he croaked: "Oliver."

Oliver dropped to the floor. "Hey." He did his best to offer a smile, his anger forgotten. "It's okay."

Dean looked sheepishly at him, then down at his own hands, at the blotchy, pale-and-purple skin, at the filthy long nails. When he spoke, it was barely a whisper: "What happened to me?"

"I'm pretty sure you're a zombie," Oliver replied.

"Zombie," Dean repeated, and he almost chuckled. "Huh. So, I'm really still dead?"

"Yeah," Oliver replied, "undead, really. You know, dead, but — not."

Dean sighed. "I knew it."

Oliver wondered what to say. Dean didn't sound too happy about this. Oliver thought about pointing out that, really, it was an improvement over being just dead.

Then again, maybe Dean was missing being alive. Oliver could kind of relate to that.

"Come on," said Oliver, patting Dean on the shoulder. "Let's get out of here."

"All right."

They ducked out the door and down Twilight Lane.

"How long have you been back?" Oliver asked.

"About two weeks, I think," Dean mumbled, his head hung low.

"You have some supernatural powers now," Oliver offered, trying to cheer him up. "You can probably jump farther and stuff." In the brief time Oliver had known the living Dean, he had seemed like a hard-luck kid. Not so coordinated, kind of scared of things — maybe being a zombie would be better for him.

"Guess," Dean muttered.

"There's other cool zombie stuff," Oliver added. "Um . . . fire doesn't hurt you, and you'll never die —"

"I just did."

"Well, right . . . you know what I mean. Zombies are more eternal than vampires." Oliver stopped there, deciding not to mention that zombies could easily be destroyed by having their heads chopped off or being dropped into a vat of salt, or the more disturbing fact that because of all the skin decay and bacterial problems that zombies usually had, the older ones ended up being merely skeletons.

They walked downhill through dark, rain-swept streets until they reached the canal. They sat on the grass at the edge of the black water, a high bridge arcing above them. Out on the water, a long sailboat cruised by, lit with strings of golden lights. Warm silhouettes frolicked about on the deck, laughing and talking.

"How did I die?" Dean asked quietly, staring into space.

"Don't you . . . remember?" Oliver asked tentatively.

"Not really." Dean's brow worked. "I remember we were at school. You were there, after chorus practice, I think? Something happened. . . . Then it's all blank, until I woke up in my —" His voice got quiet. "In my coffin."

Oliver couldn't help feeling a wave of relief. The truth of how Dean died was still a mystery, but at least Dean didn't think Oliver did it, like Emalie did. And Oliver didn't plan on changing that. "You were killed by a vampire," Oliver said carefully. "My brother, or maybe one of his friends, I'm pretty sure. . . . I got knocked out in the craziness. I — I don't know exactly how it happened," Oliver finished. *Nice job,* he thought darkly. *You managed not to lie.*

"Huh," said Dean.

Oliver hoped he wouldn't ask *why* he'd been killed. That would be a longer trip around the truth, or would Oliver just say: *You were killed because of me?*

Luckily, Dean didn't ask. "I had to dig my way out," he muttered, looking at his hands again. "I can't get the dirt off."

Oliver wondered at this. Vampire children didn't have to dig out of graves since they were born in labs. Sired vampires did, but Phlox and Sebastian had probably just buried Oliver lightly somewhere, maybe even in the house, since he had been so small. Still, a vampire would never sound upset about this kind of thing, like Dean did, but zombies didn't have the awareness that vampires had.

Most vampires, once they felt the power of forces around them, thought of being undead as an improvement, not only over being dead but also over being alive. Though zombies could use the forces, too, they didn't have that higher sense of the universe, of the many parallel worlds that mingled with this one. And zombies weren't inhabited by demons. Vampires used these reasons, and zombies' typically awful smell, as excuses to look down on them. They weren't allowed into vampire establishments unless as servants, and even then, as Oliver had seen in the Underground, it was frowned upon. Usually they were used at home, or in war. Some particularly powerful vampires had raised entire armies of zombies, or housekeeping staffs and gardeners and such. They made excellent help because they were mystically bonded to the will of their master —

Wait a minute. "Dean," Oliver began, "who raised you?"

"What?" Dean looked up quizzically.

"Do you know who your master is?"

Dean just blinked at him. "You mean somebody brought me back like this on purpose?"

"Well, yeah."

Dean looked down at his hands again and chuckled darkly. "I don't know."

Oliver felt a tremor of worry. He was pretty sure that, normally, a master would have immediately identified himself to his zombie servant. There would be no reason to let a zombie just wander around when he could be getting to work. *Unless,* Oliver thought, *the master didn't want the zombie, or anybody else, to know his identity.* Could a master control a zombie from afar? Oliver would need to find out. Was Dean being controlled right now? Oliver glanced at Dean warily. It didn't seem like it. . . .

"Who," Dean muttered, "would do this?"

"Well, it's probably one of your relatives or something." Oliver tried to sound upbeat. He wasn't feeling that way inside, but until he could find out more about the master-zombie relationship, it seemed like he should try to help Dean adjust, rather than freak him out more. "I mean, maybe they're waiting for the right time to tell you, so you're not overwhelmed."

"*Mmm*," Dean grunted.

Oliver decided to leave the topic. Dean seemed unhappy enough. Telling him that he was likely somebody's servant probably hadn't helped. "I can get you something to clean your hands," he said instead. Most of what was on Dean's hands wasn't actually dirt but mold and bacterial blooms. Vampires had products for that. And there were creams for hiding skin rot, though nothing truly strong enough for zombies, who got it way worse.

"Thanks," Dean said.

Oliver tried to think of what else to say. "You've done a good job with the — the smell."

"Oh, right." Dean almost smiled. "Yeah, that's my mom. She's *obsessed* with that."

Oliver was surprised by this. "Your parents know you're back?"

"Yeah," Dean said. "I mean, where else was I supposed to go after I dug out?"

"Well . . ." Oliver was pretty sure that most zombies would have gone straight downtown and found other zombies to live with. Zombies tended to dwell in large pods, usually in abandoned tunnels or warehouses, though Oliver had heard that there was a particularly large pod beneath the Seahawks stadium. Zombies were huge fans of rough sports like American football and pro wrestling, which vampires wanted little to do with.

"My parents were a little freaked out at first," Dean said matter-of-factly. "My brother was okay with it, my sister not so much . . . but my dad tried to kill me with a pitchfork." He rubbed his shoulder. "That hurt."

"Ouch," Oliver offered.

Dean huffed. "I know, right? My mom just screamed and cried for a couple days, but now they're kind of coming around."

"That's nice," said Oliver. "It's nice that you have them."

"Yeah," Dean agreed. "Mom's been all about helping me mask the smell, and she's done a ton of research, you know, on things like sand baths, so my skin decay doesn't get worse. And she's been trying, with the meals. She buys whole animals now, so I can have the . . ."

"Brains," Oliver finished.

"Yeah." Dean sighed. "And organs, too. Raw. She's getting all into which kinds are the healthiest."

"My mom's like that, too."

Dean sighed. "Thing is, she's not very good at preparing them, yet, so . . ."

"So you've been getting food from our place."

"Sorry."

"It's fine," said Oliver.

"On the bright side, I guess we can hang out more." Dean offered Oliver a hopeful look.

"Yeah," Oliver agreed. *How's that going to look?* he wondered. From hanging out with humans to hanging out with zombies. Yet he *had* gotten Dean killed — maybe it was the least he could do. And he didn't really have anyone else he wanted to hang out with these days. "But shouldn't you be hanging out with other zombies?" Oliver asked.

"Oh, yeah." Dean's face fell. "*Them.* I don't know. I mean, my parents let me go out at night. They want me to make some friends, but . . ."

"You've been coming to my house instead," Oliver finished.

"Yeah. I didn't know where else I could go and just, you know, be. Oh . . ." Dean rummaged in his coat and produced the newspaper clipping. "I'm sorry I took this," he said, handing it back to Oliver. "I just liked the picture." It was Dean's obituary, with his smiling school picture above it.

Silence passed over them. Oliver looked up and found a bat weaving among the bridge rafters.

"Now I guess we just have to get Emalie to quit school and start staying up all night, right?" Dean said, again with that hopeful tone.

Oliver halted. "Um, does she — does she know you're back?"

Dean sighed. "No. I was thinking once I'd talked to you that maybe it would be easier if we went together.

That way you could help her understand that I'm not dangerous?"

"Mmm . . ." *'Cause she'd really trust me on that subject*, thought Oliver.

"Hey, we should go see her now," said Dean enthusiastically. "It's almost dawn. We could wake her up and —"

"Ooh, um, let's wait," Oliver interrupted, his thoughts racing. "I haven't actually seen her since you died."

"Really? Why not?"

"Well . . ." Oliver wondered what to say next. "She was pretty upset about losing you. She didn't really want to see anyone. I've been trying to give her space."

"But now I'm back!" Dean's eyes lit up. "Come on, let's just go spring it on her. She'll probably think it's cool!"

Oliver was so tempted by the idea. "How about," he said carefully, "we go check in on her first, you know, see how she's doing? And wait until she looks like she's in a really good mood. 'Cause, you know, it's a lot to take, meeting a zombie, even if it's you."

"You mean spy on her?" Dean eyed Oliver sideways.

"W-well —" Oliver stammered. "Not really spying. More just watching —"

But Dean just shrugged. "Sure," he said. "Sounds like a plan." The idea might have bothered a human, but not a zombie, even a reluctant one. "How about tomorrow night?"

Oliver felt a surge of excitement and worry at once. "All right."

They sat for another minute.

"Hey, check it out," Dean said finally.

Oliver followed his pointing arm toward Capitol Hill, to the east. The sky was shading from black to gray.

"Time for bed, for us nocturnal creatures," Dean said almost happily, patting Oliver on the back. "Hey, your name: Nocturne. I get that now."

Oliver nodded, feeling awkward and yet fine. This was fine. Zombie Dean . . .

They stood up. "See you tomorrow night, then?" Dean said.

"Yeah," said Oliver. "See ya." He started home, then turned and watched Dean stalk off into the shadows. Dean was back. The only question was: Why?

CHAPTER 3

Stalking

Early the next evening, Oliver awoke with a start, a strange dream fresh in his mind. He was with Dean and Emalie, walking down the school halls. Dean was a zombie. It was one of those weird, jumbled worlds around them. The spray-painted neon grotesqua was glowing on the walls, but sunlight that seemed too red streamed in through the windows. And the floor was made of grass. Standing on either side of them were Oliver's classmates, leering silently. Despite that, Oliver, Emalie, and Dean were joking around, until they reached the door to the gym. . . .

Dean reached forward and pushed it open. "*I'm going to find out, you know,*" he said to Oliver with a smile.

Inside, they found everyone else from the night of Dean's death, standing frozen in place. The kids were huddled together. The Emalie and Dean from that night were with them. Bane and his friends Ty and Randall were there, too.

"*Everyone, take your places,*" said the Emalie standing with Oliver. She was dressed in black and seemed to be standing in a shadow. Oliver couldn't tell where it was coming from. It was like the lights had been dimmed, but only around her.

"*Come on, Oliver,*" Dean said, lying down on the floor.

Suddenly the dream blurred and Oliver was about to bite Dean, his face inches away from Dean's neck. Oliver could hear the blood pumping — "*Oliver, no!*" Dean screamed.

Oliver struggled to look to the door, where Banc's friend Randall was keeping guard. "*No!*" Oliver shouted. "*Just hold on! I don't kill you, that's not what happens!*"

But then Oliver heard the echoing, ancient voice of Illisius in his head: "*Oliver, don't fight it, my boy. It's time. . . .*"

"*Freeze it right there!*" Emalie ordered.

Things blurred again, and Oliver found himself suspended in midair above the scene, except his body was also below, still on top of Dean.

"*Where are you going?*" Emalie asked, looking up at him, annoyed.

"*To Nexia,*" Oliver said calmly. Looking up, he saw that the ceiling had been replaced by a pure black sky with liquid constellations and huge planets.

"*Have a nice trip!*" Dean called, waving, no longer upset.

"*No,*" Emalie said sternly. She had her arms out in front of her, and almost looked like she was pressing against the air. "*It's right here,*" she said, grimacing. "*There's something . . . but I can't . . . What are you?*" she shouted into space. As she did so, that shadow seemed to wrap around her again, like a cloud or something was clinging to her, but she didn't seem to notice it.

"*Oliver, check it out,*" Dean called. "*You killed me.*" Oliver looked down to find Dean lying on the floor alone. His neck had two red holes. Blood seeped across the floor.

"*No!*" Oliver shouted. "*I didn't do that!*"

Emalie looked up at him darkly. "*Yes you did. You do it every time. We all see it.*"

Oliver looked around to find every other person in the room staring at him coldly. "*No!*" he shouted.

"No!"

Oliver's eyes snapped open. He was in bed. There was no starry sky overhead, just the white satin fabric of his coffin lid. He looked down to see that he'd tossed and turned himself out of his sleeping soil, but his shivers weren't coming from the cold. . . .

It only took him a moment to realize that sleep wasn't returning anytime soon. He listened, and when he heard only silence, he reached to the side of his coffin and grasped a polished wooden handle. The bolts that kept his coffin lid locked slid open with a series of quiet clicks.

All coffins still locked from the inside, with the exception of those for newborns, which could be locked externally. Vampires usually slept deeply, and the daylight hours of slumber had traditionally been the best time for humans to stake them. This rarely if ever happened anymore, but coffins were still sold based not just on comfort (features like soil humidity regulation, satin interior thread count) but also safety (triple-bolt locks, fire-resistant finishes, garlic-proof odor seals). Oliver and his family had midlevel Morlock Tempurpedic coffins, from the SlumberStill series. The next line up, the HomeMausoleum, even had video surveillance and wireless servant-summoning technology.

Oliver's lid quietly yawned open. He sat up, brushing a last bit of warm sleeping soil off his legs, then hopped down to the stone floor. Phlox and Sebastian's coffin was silent beside his, Bane's as well beyond that. The crypt was barely lit by tiny crimson magmalight nightlights at the base of each wall.

Oliver turned and knelt. His coffin was at waist height. Beneath it were two rows of dresser drawers. He opened the bottom one and rummaged through his school uniform shirts until his hands closed on a small object. It was a jewelry box made of ivory, its edges lined with pewter. Sebastian had given Phlox a necklace in it. Oliver flipped open the box. Inside was a jumbled little trio of objects. Oliver brushed them out into an orderly row: the teardrop earring, the green hair elastic, and the crumpled note. They still smelled faintly of Emalie. He had to find a way to prove that he hadn't killed Dean. . . . *Unless I really did,* he thought worriedly. That dream had made it seem like he really had. And what could he do now, anyway? Weeks ago, he'd searched through Bane's drawers and found no trace of that turquoise orb that he'd had with him that night. What other evidence was there? It seemed to be just his word against everyone else's.

Soon he climbed back into his coffin, and much later the endless Saturday was finally through. Oliver trudged upstairs for breakfast. Bane was still asleep and Sebastian was gone. Phlox was on the phone when he entered the kitchen.

"I see. Well, *I'll* say that's strange. No — Francyne, no. You should stay home. I can get down there. It's no problem."

Oliver sat at the kitchen island and found a goblet waiting for him, along with a pill of crushed herbs. He scowled at the pill, but forced it down as usual.

"All right," Phlox continued, "I'll let you know what I find out. Mm-bye." She hung up.

"Hey, Mom."

"Oh." Phlox almost jumped. "Oliver, I didn't hear you come up."

"Sorry."

"No." Phlox glanced distractedly around the kitchen. "That's all right. Listen, I have to go out for a bit. That was Francyne on the phone. I'll be back maybe around midnight."

"Okay." Oliver noted the worry in Phlox's voice. "What's going on?"

"Nothing, it's — it's nothing to worry about, just a quick meeting of Central Council." She hurried about, filling her shoulder bag.

"Sounds serious," said Oliver.

"Yeah, well, gotta run." Phlox rushed toward the stairs. "Your father's at work all night, so . . ." She looked back at him, her brow furrowing with concern. "You don't have any plans to leave, do you?"

"Nah," Oliver lied.

"Okay, that's good." Surprisingly, she left it at that and disappeared down the stairs.

Oliver drained his goblet. He was glad that whatever was worrying Phlox wasn't him for once. Still, his mom wasn't the biggest fan of Central Council, the main body of vampire government in the city. She often said that she couldn't wait to end her term as eighth district liaison. So it was definitely strange to see her rushing out on a Saturday.

But it made Oliver's life easier, as he immediately left for Emalie's before Bane woke up.

He headed across town through a light rain. The city was dreary and dark. The holiday lights were long gone, and it had rained at least a little for, like, thirty straight days. That kind of thing was always hard on the humans. They started acting strange, desperate, some even jumping off bridges. Oliver could hear them carousing now, an extra-crazed edge to their voices, as he passed a row of bars. Neon signs lit the raindrops and leafless trees.

As he walked, his thoughts returned to that strange dream. What kept bothering Oliver was the way that Emalie seemed to be controlling the action. If dreams were supposed to be your subconscious telling you something, then what did that mean? It didn't make sense.

He emerged from his thoughts as he reached Emalie's house. He stopped, looking up nervously. It had been very hard not to come here before now. The last five weeks, Oliver had thought about it every night, but had kept reminding himself: *She doesn't want to see you. She thinks you're a monster.* Yet here he was.

A quiet, scraping sound broke the silence. Oliver turned to find Dean stepping out of the shadows. He was holding a chicken bone and grinding it down with his teeth. Bones, especially the marrow, were a normal part of a zombie's diet. Oliver had once walked by an entire pod grinding like that in the Underground, and the sound had been deafening.

"Hey," said Oliver.

Dean nodded. He glanced warily up at the little house. "Maybe she's already asleep." He sounded almost hopeful.

Oliver led the way up the brick steps of the walkway through the overgrown yard. The front porch was dark. A light shone weakly from the living room. Oliver wondered how Emalie's dad was doing. The few times Oliver had ever seen him, he hadn't looked well. And he'd been talking to Margie, Emalie's mother, as if she were in the house, when she'd been missing for two years.

Oliver glanced to the single upstairs window, which was also dark. Emalie's room. He could still picture himself lying on her floor, the night before Dean had died, when he had been on the run. There was so much that Oliver had found out in those days before Longest Night, yet it had almost seemed like a dream in the weeks since, when there had been nothing else to do except get back to life as usual. But now, being here, he remembered the feeling: knowing that his parents, his vampire parents, had been lying to him about his whole life (*Aren't they still?* he reminded himself). He'd felt safe in Emalie's room that night. Normal. He'd actually slept well on her floor.

"Let's check the basement." Dean was stepping past Oliver with surprising decisiveness.

Oliver followed him around the house to the small window, just above the ground. There was red light spilling from it. They peered in carefully, but found Emalie's darkroom area empty. There were no photo supplies out, no trays of chemicals in the sink, nor photos hanging up. Oliver remembered now that Emalie's camera had gotten damaged in the Underground. There was only a stack of books on the floor. They looked old, their bindings frayed. A beat-up spiral notebook was lying open on top of the pile.

"Maybe she's in the kitchen," Dean whispered, starting toward the back of the house.

Oliver lingered, looking in at the darkroom space, its walls still made of unpacked boxes. Almost as if on cue, his side ached. It had been on that concrete floor that the amulet had shattered and showed him his true parents. He remembered the portal vision now with a rush of sadness — remembered Emalie in it with him, sensed her scent there —

Wait, no, her scent wasn't in the vision. It was here now.

"Dean!" Dean was just reaching the side of the house when Oliver grabbed him by the shoulders and lunged forward. They flew up over a van parked in the back alley. As they landed, Oliver pushed Dean to the ground.

"Ow! What the —"

"*Tssss*," Oliver hissed quietly.

Just then, the basement door of Emalie's house squealed. Watching through the narrow space beneath the van, they saw the door open. Emalie appeared. She was wearing a black wool sweater and a black knit hat, and had a backpack slung over her shoulder. She crept away from the house and stole off down the alley.

"What's she doing?" Dean asked as they watched her go.

"Come on," Oliver said and started off after her.

CHAPTER 4

The Sunlight Slaying

They hadn't gone ten feet when Emalie froze. Oliver grabbed Dean and pulled him to the side of a garage as Emalie slowly looked over her shoulder. She stared down the alley for a moment, then turned and kept moving.

"That was close," said Dean. He started back out into the alley.

"Wait." Oliver held him back. "Let's let her go for a while. I can keep track of her."

They let a minute pass, then leaped to the roof of the garage and bounded from one rooftop to the next. Dean was not quite able to land as quietly on the sleeping houses as Oliver could, his feet thudding on each roof. "Sorry," he offered before Oliver had said anything.

They angled across the neighborhood, leaping over yards and streets. Oliver tried to track Emalie on the wind, but her scent seemed more faint than usual, so they had to stay close, keeping her in sight, but not too close, such that she'd hear Dean's landings.

Emalie reached a thickly wooded park and disappeared beneath the trees. Oliver and Dean hopped down to the sidewalk and followed cautiously after her. The park yawned down a gentle hill. Large old pines shrouded the sparse grass beneath. Here and there, lampposts cast cones of white light on the cement walkways that twisted through the darkness.

"There," Oliver whispered. He pointed down to their right. Emalie was in a very dark gathering of trees, kneeling in the grass, her bag in front of her. "Can you tell what she's up to?"

"Nah," Dean replied, squinting. "It's kinda dark for photos, though, isn't it?"

"We should get closer," Oliver suggested.

"Closer?" said Dean. "She might see us!"

Oliver felt a twinge of his old annoyance with Dean. He was still nervous, even as a zombie. "Not too close," Oliver said, and was just about to start forward when a sound made him stop.

"What was that?" whispered Dean.

It had sounded like laughter, coming from the other direction. "This way," said Oliver. They crept away through the trees and spied a small sandy playground. There were three figures there. They looked young.

"Vampires. Stay here," Oliver said sternly. "And, Dean, I mean it."

"Fine with me," Dean agreed, sounding not at all hurt to be left behind.

Oliver walked down through the shadows, glancing to his right as he did so. He couldn't see Emalie from here, and the wind was blowing uphill, but if it shifted at all it could carry her scent to these vampires. Now he heard one of them talking:

"And he was so scared. It was like he'd never seen a Norwegian Mongreloid before!" Oliver recognized the voice as it went on. "What a freak."

One of the others chuckled.

Oliver dropped down onto the sand, shoving his hands into his sweatshirt pockets as he walked closer. The vampires looked up.

"Is that Oliver Nocturne?"

"Theo," Oliver said simply.

Oliver's classmate, Theo Moore, was lounging across the top bars of a jungle gym. His friends Brent and Maggots were sitting on the spring-powered seesaw, rocking up and down a little, but they stopped the moment they saw Oliver.

"What are you doing out so late?" Theo asked. He spoke with that same sarcastic tone that he'd used to pick on Oliver in the past, except these days he sounded just a bit less certain. Everyone at school looked at Oliver differently since he'd allegedly killed Dean. Oliver didn't enjoy it. He felt like a curiosity: like a leopard at the zoo — everyone watching him through glass and wondering what he might do next. It was kind of nice not to be made fun of, but Oliver felt like it was only a matter of time before he screwed it up. So lately he'd been saying as little as possible. That way, maybe everyone would think he was mysterious, when really, he didn't know what to say.

"I'm just out," Oliver said now, and an awkward silence passed over the three. The wind shifted downhill, and Oliver caught a faint scent of Dean. He noticed Maggots cocking his head strangely as well, but then the breeze died down. "What are you doing here?" Oliver asked.

"We're looking for humans," Theo said, still with some attitude, but also with that ever-so-slight edge of defensiveness. "Not to *make friends* with, either," Theo added.

"What's that supposed to mean?" Oliver shot back.

Theo looked hard at Oliver for a moment. In the past, Theo would definitely have said something mean right here — but he just shook his head. "Nothing. What are *you* doing here?"

"Same thing."

"Huh." Theo shrugged. He sat up, and when he spoke again, his tone had lost some of its edge. "Not a lot of action with this rain, though."

"Nah," Oliver agreed.

"Boo," Maggots said disappointedly. Brent just eyed Oliver.

The wind picked up again, rustling wet pine trees. It had shifted slightly, probably not enough, but Oliver glanced in the direction where Emalie had been —

A figure was lurking in the shadows. Was that her? The figure looked about her height, but now disappeared behind a tree. Oliver peered into the dark. . . . Suddenly the figure darted back out. Something flashed orange from him or her, like the burst of a match being lit, only larger and brighter —

Oliver heard a sizzling sound and felt a wave of warm energy pass over him. It came and went in an instant.

"What was that?" Theo was spinning around toward the trees, but the figure was gone. He turned to Oliver. "Did you see something?"

Oliver shrugged. "See what?"

"Hey," Maggots said from beside them.

Theo narrowed his eyes at Oliver. "Are you up to something, Nocturne?"

"Hey!" Maggots said more urgently.

Oliver and Theo turned. Maggots was staring at Brent, who was still sitting on the seesaw.

"Nnnn," Brent moaned. He was bent over the handle.

"What's with him?" Theo asked.

"Nnnnnnn . . ." Brent rocked back and forth.

"What's happening to him?" Maggots asked worriedly.

Brent was starting to glow. There seemed to be a faint aura of golden light around him —

"Nnnnnnnaaaaaaaaa!" He lurched off the seesaw, collapsing to his knees in the sand. His face was contorted, eyes shut, fangs bared.

"B-Brent?" Theo stammered.

"Aaaaaaaaaaaaaaaaaah!" Brent's head whipped up. His eyes popped open and brilliant, blazing light shot out. Now it burst from his mouth, too. His head thrashed about, and when the light hit Oliver, he felt an unmistakable sting and leaped backward in panic. It felt exactly like —

"Sunlight!" Theo shouted, grabbing at his chest. His shirt was on fire where the light had hit him. Oliver looked down to see that his sweatshirt was singed. "Run!" Theo vaulted off the jungle gym and sprinted for the nearby trees. Maggots fell over himself, tumbling to the sand and crawling beneath the seesaw.

Oliver stumbled back. Brent staggered to his feet, the light from his eyes, mouth, and ears arcing about as he shook his head. Now his chest was beginning to glow.

The beams swept by Oliver and the leg of his pants caught fire. There was searing pain. He tried to run —

"*Tsss!*" His side suddenly seized up on him. The pain from his amulet wound shot like a spear up and down his side. He lost control of his legs and fell to the sand.

There was humming, buzzing light everywhere in the night. Oliver felt heat on his back and managed to roll over, his side screaming in pain. Brent was floundering in his direction, sunlight bursting from every inch of his body now as his skin seemed to crack open. The light overwhelmed him, and he became only an outline in a tiny supernova. It grew brighter and more intense, and Brent's features were lost completely. . . .

Then it went dark.

Oliver blinked back blindness. He slapped at his legs and torso, putting out small fires on his clothes. As the green spots in his eyes faded, he saw only a lingering wisp of smoke where Brent had been.

Maggots walked slowly over. He kicked at the sand beneath where Brent had stood. Fine silver ash scattered about. Brent had been turned to dust.

"Dude," Maggots said weakly. "Brent?" He stared at the ground, then looked at Oliver. "What was that?" Vampires were not ones to get too saddened when another was dusted. Given time, though, they could get very angry about it. Revenge was a popular idea in the vampire world and was considered a healthy thing to do every now and then. For now, though, Maggots just seemed confused.

Oliver pulled himself to his knees, his side burning. "I don't know." He glanced back at the trees. Whatever it was had come from that direction, and inside, he felt a horrible, freezing worry: *Emalie* . . .

Suddenly something shrieked in the sky above. Oliver and Maggots looked up to see a large bat circling down through the trees. Now a horned owl swooped over, and a crow. There was rustling nearby, and Oliver saw a raccoon bounding toward them, then a coyote. Flares of black smoke began to swirl around the animals — and adult vampires were leaping down to the playground.

"Don't move! Any of you!" a booming voice called.

In moments, Oliver and Maggots were surrounded.

CHAPTER 5

The Scourge of Selket

There were five figures ringing the sand playground. Three women and two men, all in long black coats. On their lapels were gleaming pins made of bone, carved in the shape of a Skrit symbol that Oliver didn't recognize.

Oliver stood up quickly.

"What happened?" asked a short woman. She had dark skin, frizzy hair, and red eyes.

"Brent," Maggots mumbled, pointing at the sand.

The woman glanced down at the ash, then to Maggots. "Did you see what caused this?"

"We were just sitting here," Maggots added.

A narrow man wearing a high black turtleneck sweater beneath his coat stepped forward and knelt in the sand. He had curly black hair and wore small, round glasses. He produced a glass ball, which he flipped open and used to scoop up a sample of the ash.

"How about you?"

Oliver looked up to find the woman peering at him. "What?" Oliver said.

"What happened here?"

"I, um, I saw . . ." Oliver had only a second to decide how much he would say. "I just saw Brent light up. Before that, I felt a flash of energy or something."

"Do you know where it came from?" the woman asked, her eyes narrowing.

"No." Oliver cursed at himself inside. Lying again . . . But he felt like he had to. Had Emalie just done this? Why would she? *Maybe because she saw a vampire kill her cousin,* he thought. True, there was that. Oh, this was not good.

"You didn't see anything else?" the woman asked, sounding unconvinced.

"I don't know." Again, Oliver tried to talk in truths without details rather than outright lies. "We were just talking when it happened. Me and Theo, and —"

"Are you Theo?" the woman asked Maggots.

"This one is," a male voice called from across the playground. Oliver looked over to see Theo walking back toward them, being followed by another black-coated vampire —

It was Sebastian. "Hey, Ollie," he said. "Are the rest of you all right?"

"Yeah," Oliver replied, more than a little confused. "Just some burns."

Sebastian turned to the short woman. "Leah, is the area secure?"

Leah closed her eyes. She held her arms out, tilting her palms up and down. The air began to ripple like liquid around them. "There's a zombie a hundred meters northwest and a, wait —" She squinted, reading the resonance of invisible forces. "A human leaving the park — ah, no, sorry, that's a false reading." She opened her eyes. "The area's secure."

Sebastian turned to the man who had scooped the ash. "What do we have, Tyrus?"

Tyrus placed the glass ball in the center of a small square gadget. It began spinning in a curved depression. "Well," Tyrus read grimly from a blue screen, "the burning and vitamin D residuals are consistent with the other incidents. What do you think, Yasmin?"

"It's the Scourge," Yasmin, a woman wearing a white head scarf, murmured darkly.

"What's going on?" Theo asked impatiently.

Oliver watched as the vampires checked with one another silently and felt his own frustration building. He was becoming far too used to trying to read into the faces of those who were keeping him in the dark.

"It's nothing to be worried about," said Sebastian.

"But my friend just got dusted!" Theo went on, his voice edged with fear. "We need to know what's going on."

Oliver found that he agreed with Theo. If he was right about what he'd felt moments ago, whatever had dusted Brent had barely missed him.

"We're looking into it," Tyrus said firmly. "That's all you need to know right now. We'll escort you home, and if your parents have questions, tell them to contact Mr. Ravonovich at the Half-Light Consortium." He turned and stalked off into the trees. The raccoon was waiting obediently there and, with a swirl of smoke, he Occupied it and scurried off.

Leah took Maggots by the arm. He was still staring vacantly down at the sand by the seesaw. "Dude," he muttered again, sounding lonely.

Yasmin led Theo away, and Sebastian moved alongside Oliver. "We should go," he said simply, putting an arm around his shoulders.

"Dad," Oliver said quietly, giving the park one more wary glance as they left, "what just happened?" The image of Brent being swallowed by sunlight kept playing in his mind, and an even worse thought occurred to him: *If Emalie did that . . . what if she'd meant it for me?*

Sebastian took a minute before answering. "Listen, I can tell you some things, but please keep them to yourself. The Central Council wants to keep any rumors from starting up, so things don't get out of hand."

"What things? What happened to Brent?"

"Well, this won't make much sense, but he was slain by sunlight. It's a mystic spell," Sebastian continued, "called the Scourge of Selket. Our historians have pinpointed its origin in the ancient Egyptian dynasty of Amenemhet I. Peasants used it in a revolt against the pharaoh and his bureaucracy, which was controlled by vampires. Selket was a protective goddess, and they harnessed her power to infect the vampires with sunlight, destroying them from the inside out. Historians think the Orani were involved."

"Huh," Oliver muttered, a shiver passing over him as he remembered that Dead Désirée had referred to Emalie as an Orani, part of a secret line of women who had *sight*.

"Yeah," Sebastian continued, "except that no vampire had been slain by the Scourge in over two thousand years . . . until this week."

They left the park and continued down a silent street. A light mist began to fall. The pain in Oliver's side had calmed, but there was still a faint burning there.

"So," Oliver asked, "Brent wasn't the first to get attacked by this Scourge?"

"No," Sebastian said. "He was the third. Both the others were kids, too. The first one was over in Capitol Hill. The boy's dad had a home lab for rot leeches, so when we heard that somebody self-combusted, we assumed it was an accident with the flame incubators for that. But then the second was just a kid at a convenience store in Madrona . . . and now this."

"Nobody's been talking about it at school or anything," Oliver mused.

"We've been keeping it out of the news," Sebastian said.

"Who were those people you were with?"

"They work with me at Half-Light," Sebastian replied.

"They were all lawyers?"

"Ha, no." Sebastian laughed. "I'm the only attorney." He didn't add anything further.

It occurred to Oliver that he really didn't know what the Half-Light Consortium did. Sebastian had described his job as being there to get Half-Light out of legal trouble when they were doing whatever *else* they did. *One thing they do is keep an eye on me,* Oliver reminded himself. That was something he still needed to try to find out about. But his dad always managed to talk about his job and Half-Light without giving any details. Oliver tried to think of a question for him now, to get more information —

But suddenly Sebastian halted, throwing an arm in front of him. "*Shhh.*" He looked warily up at the rooftops, sniffing the air.

"What is it?" Oliver asked.

They were in the middle of a well-lit intersection. Something scraped above them.

"Who's there?!" Sebastian roared through the darkness. Oliver saw a silhouette atop a four-story apartment building. The figure spun around to flee —

"Whoa —" But instead slipped and toppled off the edge. He fell four stories and slammed to the pavement with an awful thud. "Buh," the figure moaned, slowly getting to his feet. Oliver saw who it was and sagged. "Hey, Oliver," Dean said groggily. He limped toward them, dragging one leg behind him. "I think I broke something."

"Who's this?" Sebastian asked, sounding confused.

Oliver wondered if there was any way he could pretend he didn't know Dean. No, it would never work. So, what could he say about his zombie friend?

"Isn't that the boy you killed?" Sebastian asked quietly, that uncertain tone that had been so common in December returning to his voice. Luckily, he'd asked too softly for Dean to hear.

"Yes," Oliver muttered.

Oliver felt Sebastian's gaze fall on him. He glanced up, having no idea what to expect, and was shocked to be greeted by a wide smile. "Ollie, this is amazing. You — wow . . . Oh, I'm sorry." He turned to Dean. "I'm Sebastian Nocturne, Oliver's father."

"Hi," Dean said nervously. "Hey, Oliver, are you all right? What happened back there?"

Oliver wanted to ask Dean what he had seen, but he knew he had to save it for later. "I'm fine. We don't really know what happened."

"How long have you been risen?" Sebastian asked curiously, gazing at Dean in wonder.

Dean looked at him confusedly. "Huh? Oh, right, like from the grave. About two weeks."

Sebastian nodded to himself, like he was counting in his head. "Right, of course. You'd have to lie dead for one lunar cycle before you could be raised. . . ." He glanced at Oliver again with a look of amazement. Oliver had thought Sebastian would be disappointed in him for having a zombie as a friend, but now he understood: *He thinks I raised Dean*. That was the logical explanation, if you thought that Oliver had killed Dean to begin with. Well, this could work in Oliver's favor, but he had to get Dean out of here. Oliver still needed to explain this stuff to him.

"Dean, we have to get home," he said quickly. "Meet me after school on Monday, okay?"

"Cool." Dean nodded. "Nice to meet you," he added to Sebastian, and started limping off in the other direction, wincing. "See ya later," he called.

Oliver and Sebastian returned home. They were just

< 57 >

entering the kitchen when Sebastian called excitedly, "Phlox, you won't believe it."

Phlox was chopping sugarcane at the counter. She looked up quickly. "You're all right. . . ." Her face relaxed into a smile. "What happened?"

Bane was sitting at the island, dumping a can of Jolt into a French press cup of coffee, while popping chocolate-coated cicada larvae into his mouth. He looked up, saw Oliver's sullen face, and his eyes lit up with excitement. "Is he in trouble?" he asked like a hopeful vulture. He removed the press and drank the concoction with the coffee grounds still in it.

"Ollie turned his first kill into a servant!" Sebastian announced proudly.

Phlox gazed at Oliver with wide eyes. "Honey, really?"

"I . . ." Oliver started. He narrowed his eyes at Bane, wondering: *Did you do this, too?*

But Bane's eyes only returned a look of pure bitterness.

"The prodigy continues to impress!" Sebastian patted Oliver on the shoulder. "And you should hear the way Ollie talks to him. Making his commands sound like choices . . ."

Bane slid off his chair and slunk out of the room.

Oliver listened helplessly as yet another lie spun out

of his control. He gave up. It was like no matter what he did, it led to some new lie. He wanted to scream: *I didn't do any of it! I'm not a prodigy!* Right now he should have been getting punished for all these things that kept happening. At least that would have made *sense*. But no, he was a star, and it just kept getting better, and yet worse at the same time.

"Unbelievable," Phlox said. "Oliver, a zombie raising? That is so difficult!" Her eyes gleamed with pride. "How did you learn to do that?"

"I don't know," he finally muttered. "You know, I just did."

"I can't think of any other vampires," Phlox went on, "who were masters at such a young age."

"He followed us halfway home from the park like a loyal dog." Sebastian beamed.

Phlox's gaze darkened. "The park . . . so what happened there?"

"Another attack," Sebastian confirmed ominously. "It was the Astors' kid: Brent."

"Did you catch anyone?"

"No," Sebastian muttered, "but we will."

Oliver headed downstairs, his thoughts distracted. At least if his parents thought he was Dean's master, they wouldn't mind the two of them hanging out. But if Dean found out Oliver's parents thought this, then

Dean would also learn the popular belief that Oliver had killed him. Oliver sighed. This was going to be tough to manage. And yet none of that was as worrisome as what had just happened at the park, and the question of whether Emalie had been involved.

CHAPTER 6

The Codex

Sunday evening, Oliver woke to find that he could barely roll over to open the lid of his coffin. He dressed slowly. With each movement, he felt a dull burning pain spreading out from his side. He headed for the bathroom and examined his amulet wound. The red, spider-webbing lines had grown. They now reached halfway across his stomach and up under his arm. Oliver couldn't believe it: They had almost doubled their reach. Maybe he did need to just tell his parents and get this taken care of. Maybe he could come up with a creative explanation for the wound, for the amulet shard. *What exactly am I going to tell them?* He had no idea.

Oliver searched among the long shelves on the wall until he found the dark glass jar of Poultice of Puffer Fish. He twisted it open and was greeted by a tangy, seawater smell. He dipped his finger into the jar and scooped out a dollop of the moist, dark brown substance. It looked almost like fruit preserves, but it was actually the mashed-up organs of the puffer fish. Deadly to eat for a living creature, puffer fish organs contained a toxin that was an excellent anesthetic for a serious vampire wound. Oliver pulled up his T-shirt and rubbed the poultice over the gash. He winced in pain — the poultice had a sharp sting at first — then felt the numbing effect take over. Oliver covered the area with a large bandage.

Upstairs, Oliver found Phlox in the living room. She was stretched out on the long black leather couch, flipping through a glossy brochure. The picture on the cover showed a volcanic eruption and streams of lava pouring into steaming seas. Across the top, it read: *Isla Necrata: Experience the Ultimate in Comfort & Chaos Vacations*.

"Hey, Oliver," she said.

"Hey," Oliver replied.

"Mom's off tonight. Grab whatever you want for breakfast."

Oliver started back into the kitchen.

"How's Dean?"

Oliver shrugged. "I don't know."

Phlox looked at him proudly. "I am still just so amazed that you made yourself a servant. How is he feeling about it?"

"Oh, um," Oliver stammered, "he hasn't really said."

"Well, sometimes zombies get a little bent out of shape. You know, they don't usually remember their death, and when they find out you killed them, they get a little cranky." Phlox sighed. "They just don't have a larger sense of the world. Anyway, they fall in line eventually."

"Mmm," Oliver said, wanting to change the subject. "Well, I'm gonna go out."

"Oh?" Phlox looked up, her fingernail frozen between pages. "Where to?"

"I don't know," Oliver said. "Maybe to the park."

"Listen, Ollie, we'd rather you stayed home today. With what happened yesterday —"

"Later, Mom." Bane's head flashed into the living room.

"All right," said Phlox, with a guilty glance at Oliver.

"We gonna string 'em up!" Bane shouted in a cowboy drawl, his voice dripping with excitement as he darted back across the kitchen. "This posse is ready to ride!" Bane's boots thudded down the stairs, and the door to the sewers slammed shut behind him.

Oliver turned to Phlox. "Why does Bane get to go out?" he asked, trying not to whine but not really succeeding.

"Oliver, the attacks have been on children," Phlox

said carefully. "Bane and his friends wanted to help with the hunt."

"Is Dad out on patrol again?"

"He'll be out all night tonight. And he wants you home."

Oliver seethed inside, but didn't see any way to argue. Knowing Bane and his friends were out there hunting as well made him worry even more about Emalie. Still, he didn't see what he could do about it. "Fine," he conceded, and headed for the TV and his video games. "I was going to go to the library tomorrow after school." He sulked. "Can I still do that?"

"Well . . ." Phlox began uncertainly, her brow furrowing.

"It's for school," Oliver lied, adding, "and the project is kind of due this week."

Then Phlox nodded resolutely. "No, okay. We'll make that happen. We can't stay holed up in fear. *Hmph*, fear . . . If your grandmother could hear me now."

Oliver could imagine Phlox's mother, Myrandah, raging in her thick Morosian accent about such a thing. There wasn't even a symbol for *fear* in Skrit. She would blame such a human emotion on the polluting effect of New World ideals and culture.

Phlox continued, "We'll make sure you can get to the library tomorrow."

"Thanks." Oliver offered a smile, but inside he kept worrying about Emalie. If she was indeed the one wielding the Scourge, Oliver hoped she wouldn't be naive enough to head out for another attack tonight. The idea of Sebastian and his Half-Light team finding her, or Bane and his posse: Neither one would end well.

✹

Oliver and Bane were on their way out the door the next evening when Phlox called: "Charles, don't forget, you're taking Oliver to the library after school."

They both froze. Oliver looked up to find Bane scowling at him. Then he smiled. "Yup." His arm flicked out, punching Oliver right on his amulet wound. Oliver stiffened in pain, trying not to show it. "No problem, Mom," Bane added, "that'll be great."

"Without the sarcasm, please," Phlox groaned.

Oliver's side ached all the way to school, but he forgot about it when he arrived. He ducked through the back door to find his schoolmates carousing on the staircase, enjoying the grotesqua that shimmered on the walls. The three-dimensional spray-painted images that obscured the cheery human murals and bulletin boards had been completely redone that week for Valentine's Day. The halls glowed bloodred and danced with scenes of romantic tragedy — demons dueling for the hand of a maiden, lovers suffering beside graves.

"Hey, Oliver!" Seth appeared beside him on the staircase. "How was your weekend? Do anything cool?"

Oliver shrugged. "Not really." Seth talking to him eagerly in the hallways was a good example of the subtle change in Oliver's world this past month. Seth and Oliver had absolutely nothing more to talk about than they used to. Except now, Oliver could feel Seth *trying*.

"I had a good weekend," Seth volunteered. "Just hanging out, playing gaaah —"

Seth was yanked out of sight. Oliver felt hands slap hard on his shoulders. "What's up, Nocturne?" Theo and Maggots appeared beside him.

"Hey," Oliver offered.

"So, Valentine's Day . . ." Theo said conspiratorially. "We boys have to stick together."

Oliver glanced at Theo. It always took him a minute to figure out what Theo was talking about, and yet it didn't feel safe to actually ask Theo: *What are you talking about?* So Oliver nodded, again hoping that his silence would be mistaken for him knowing what was going on.

"I don't know if I can stand the adoration!" Theo shouted dramatically so that everyone could hear. Then he nudged Oliver, lowering his voice. "It's going to be the worst for you, fella. Mr. First Kill and all."

"Okay." Oliver shrugged. He could feel that subtle effort from Theo now, too: trying.

"I suppose you've heard Suzyn and her friends giggling. . . ."

Oliver followed Theo's gaze down the stairs and saw Suzyn and her gaggle of friends eyeing them. Oliver was shocked to find two wide black eyes boring directly into him, belonging to the girl on Suzyn's left, Monique. She was shorter, with dark skin and a pile of braids tied back above her white collar. Oliver's eyes locked on her, and his thoughts raced with panic. Was his hair messed up? Tie crooked? Did he have cake on his chin? He turned back around immediately, tripping on the steps as he did so.

Oliver's class had Force Awareness and Manipulation first period of the evening. With a familiar sense of dread, Oliver soon found himself standing in the torchlit gymnasium, dressed in his gym uniform. The shorts. The tank top. They hung off him, only seeming to highlight the muscles he didn't have. He could almost hear the uniform mocking him: *I make you look so terrible . . . so slight.* Ms. Nikkolai, the F.A.M. teacher, insisted on uniforms, because heavy layers of clothing got in the way when climbing walls and added extra difficulty to spectralization and practicing their ceiling work, but Oliver wondered if Ms. Nikkolai might also be on a mission to crush Oliver's self-esteem completely.

The class stood in parallel lines, girls facing boys. Again, Ms. Nikkolai, who was standing in the center, claimed that this was the best way for everyone to see her — that one long line would be far too difficult to lecture to. But wasn't this really so that the girls could whisper and snicker to one another about the boys across the way? Out of the corner of his eye, Oliver saw Suzyn and Monique doing just that.

Theo leaned over from beside him. Oliver expected more jokes, but Theo was serious. "So did your dad spill any info on the Scourge?"

Oliver was surprised that Theo knew its name. Half-Light wasn't keeping as tight a lid on this as Sebastian seemed to think. "Just that Brent wasn't the first," Oliver said seriously.

"It's got to be humans, right?" said Theo. "I just hope we get another chance at them."

"They're gonna pay," Maggots muttered darkly from beside Theo.

Theo licked his lips. "You'll let us know if you hear any more. . . ."

"Um, sure," Oliver replied.

"That's enough, gentlemen," Ms. Nikkolai called from across the room, a Russian accent sharpening the tips of her words. "Nocturne, Moore, do you have a problem I should know about?" Oliver looked around to see that the rest of the class had started scaling the walls for more practice with their ceiling work. He, Theo, and Maggots scrambled to catch up.

After school, Oliver found Bane outside, leaning sulkily against the playground fence, music blaring from his headphones. As Oliver reached him, Bane just turned and started off.

"Hold on." Bane didn't stop. "Bane, hold on. We have to wait for Dean."

Bane whirled around, pulling his headphones dramatically from his ears. "Oh." He rolled his eyes. "That's right, of course, your minion. *O great Oliver, prodigy of prodigies!*"

"Well, why did you even raise him, then?!" Oliver suddenly shouted.

"Me?" Bane's eyes grew wide, and an incredulous smile spread across his face.

Oliver was so sick of these theatrics. "Yes, you, duh."

Bane's smile widened. "Oh, boy, you've got problems now. *I* didn't raise your zombie, lamb. Hasn't it been sickening enough being part of the Oliver Show since you killed him?"

"*You* killed him!"

"Oh, give it up, bro! Think about it: If I were his master, why exactly would I let him hang out with you? He'd be doing my wonderful bidding!" Bane's smile faded for a moment, as if he was contemplating this missed chance.

Oliver just stared at him. "It had to be you." But Bane had a point: He'd have found endless things to do with a zombie servant.

"Oh, just wait until Mom and Dad find out!" Bane laughed. "You know what, forget what I said. This is great. The more that gets heaped on you, the more it's going to come crashing down when everyone discovers you're a fraud! Now *that's* something to look forward to!"

"Hey, guys." Oliver turned to find Dean walking up beside them. "How's it going?"

Bane wrinkled his nose dramatically. "Oh, gross." He stalked off.

Dean's smile faltered.

"Ignore him," Oliver said. "Come on, we're going down to the library."

"Oh, cool." Dean nodded. "We're going to try to figure out who raised me?"

"Yeah," said Oliver, "and what's going on with the sunlight slayings."

"Hey," said Dean. "You don't think Emalie had something to do with that, do you?"

"Did you see her at all while it was happening?"

"Nah." Dean shook his head. "I kinda lost track of her. I couldn't find her scent or anything."

They took the tunnels downtown, emerging in a filthy alley. The trapezoidal glass facade of Seattle's Public

Library loomed over them, its windows dark. They walked to a concrete loading dock, where Oliver rapped on a steel garage door.

After a moment, boots echoed behind the door, and with a grind of metal and the hum of machinery, the door lifted. Celia St. Croix, the vampire liaison for the library, appeared. "Evenin', boys," she said brightly. "Welcome. You know where to go?"

"Yeah." Oliver nodded. He started forward.

"Hold on." Oliver turned to find Celia with a hand to Dean's chest. "It's vampires only," she said matter-of-factly to Oliver. "Help has to wait outside."

"Oh." Oliver looked at Dean uncertainly. "Sorry, I — I'll be quick. I didn't know. . . ."

"There's a Dumpster down the ways a bit," Celia offered casually to Dean.

Dean's face had fallen. "It's cool. I'm just gonna take off. Catch ya later, Oliver?"

"Okay," Oliver replied guiltily. "Meet me before school tomorrow, maybe?"

"Sure." Dean stalked off.

Oliver and Bane headed across the loading dock and through a heavy metal door. Moments later they emerged on the silent ground floor of the library, in the children's section. They crossed among low bookshelves and around tiny tables. Bane took a moment to grab a stuffed bear from one of the tables, behead it, and place it back on the chair with its head in its hands. Sometimes Oliver couldn't believe they were even brothers.

Streetlight angled in, making diamond patterns on the floor. Their footsteps echoed in the cavernous space. There were three elevators along a wall, with a fourth around a corner. Oliver and Bane walked to the middle elevator, marked #2, and pressed the DOWN button.

A loud *ding* echoed in the empty space, and the elevator doors slid open. They entered and pressed the button for the bottom floor, P. The elevator lowered. The door slid open again, revealing the concrete parking garage, but this was not where Oliver and Bane were headed. As the doors fully opened, Oliver began counting to himself in a whisper:

"One —" he said, then pressed the P button again, even though they were already on that floor. "One, two —" he counted, then pressed it again. "One, two, three, four —" He pressed it a third time. The elevator's chime rang three times, and the door slid closed. Though there were no more floors listed on the panel, the elevator began to lower.

It hummed downward for a long moment, then slid to a stop. The doors opened.

"Ahh. Welcome, Nocturnes." Before them, a wiry old vampire man dressed in a crisp tuxedo stood behind a high mahogany desk. The desk curved out from the wall of a long room.

"Hi," Oliver replied to the Librarian, not surprised that he knew them. As soon as Oliver had entered the code in the elevator, their force signatures would have been scanned and their identities verified.

The Librarian slipped out from behind his desk. "Right this way." He led them down the center of the room, its floor covered in burgundy carpet. The walls were also paneled in well-polished mahogany and lit warmly by swirling magmalight lanterns. At the end of the room was a set of black curtains. Classical music played softly. There were a few other vampires in the room, standing at small tables along the walls. "May I assist you with your search?" he asked, stopping and motioning Oliver and Bane to a free table.

"No thanks," Oliver said quickly.

Bane slouched against the wall, his music blaring, as Oliver stepped up to the small table. In the center was a silver gooseneck stand with a copper microphone at its end. A small speaker was inset in the table beside it. Oliver twisted the cone toward him, then spoke into it: "Zombie raising," he said softly.

"Eighteen," the pleasant female voice of the Catalog whispered from the speaker.

Oliver spoke again, lowering his voice and glancing quickly around: "Scourge of Selket."

"Six," the Catalog replied.

"Orani," said Oliver.

"Thirty-four," whispered the Catalog.

Oliver looked around again. Bane had discovered an attractive girl across the room. Oliver made one more request, his quietest yet: "The Nexia Gate." He saw the Librarian glance in his direction.

"Twenty-two," the Catalog whispered.

Oliver started toward the curtains, then noticed that Bane was not beside him. Glancing back, he saw that Bane was still against the wall. He had succeeded in catching the eye of the girl and was now trying to look completely uninterested.

"Please take a long time," he called sarcastically, waving Oliver away.

Oliver turned, glad that Bane wouldn't be with him. He pushed through the heavy curtain folds, stepping onto a narrow walkway of grated metal. There was a spiral staircase beside him. In front of him, a hallway ran back into darkness. To the left and right were the entrances to more hallways. The walls between these hallways were solid, made of dark wood. Footsteps echoed from floors above and below.

Oliver looked at a gold plate on the wall in front of him. An arrow pointed left beneath the numbers: 16–32. Oliver headed that way, then turned down the next aisle.

The floor and the low ceiling were still made of grated metal, but the walls on either side alternated between sets of black curtains and wood. Beside each set of curtains was a number. Oliver made his way to the curtains numbered eighteen.

"Enter," the Catalog whispered.

He pushed through the curtains, into a dark chamber lit only by a candle on each wall. Incense smoke lingered in the still, humid air, with a scent of coriander and cinnamon. There was a single pillow in the center of a small rug. Oliver sat down on it, then looked ahead into pitch-darkness.

"Zombie raising," Oliver said again.

Two glowing blue eyes lit in the dark. There was a grinding sound, and a stone pedestal slid forward. On it sat a figure shrouded in dark crimson robes, its face hidden in the shadow of a hood, except for the glowing eyes. "Continue," he said in a soft monotone voice.

Oliver paused. He'd sat with a Codex before and knew that in order to access the vast oral history it contained, he had to narrow his search by explaining what he was looking for. That required him saying things that he'd been keeping to himself. But the Codex were governed by strict confidentiality, so he didn't need to worry. *Doctors are supposed to be confidential, too,* Oliver reminded himself darkly. Well, he had little choice but to continue. "How to detect a zombie's master."

There was a deep inhalation that sounded labored,

and the sound of rattling chains. The Codex were hundreds-, sometimes thousand-year-old vampires. Only brilliant academics were chosen for the transformation. The reward was that you were kept alive eternally by enchantments and filled with the complete oral knowledge of one tome of subjects. It was an honor, but since vampires tended to regard honor as something that could be just as easily forgotten as obeyed, the Codex were shackled at the wrists and ankles. The one Oliver sat before now was particularly ancient. There were younger Codex, who were less imposing and were even brought out for story sessions with groups of vampire kids.

"A zombie's master will, with rare exceptions, be the being who killed the human," the Codex said in a hissing, labored rasp. "The zombie will perceive his master in the first moment following exhumation."

"Is there a way for a master to hide his identity?" Oliver asked.

"A master could choose not to reveal himself," the Codex answered. "There are certain enchantments, but they are difficult and rare."

"How can you discover a hidden master?"

The Codex took another deep, rattling breath. "There is a blood rite that can be performed that will mark the master, a mark that the master will not know exists, and that can be seen above all concealments."

"Explain," Oliver said. The Codex listed the steps in the ritual. Oliver listened carefully.

"Mix these ingredients in a VanMuren's Mortar," the Codex concluded, "and recite the incantation."

Oliver nodded. "Finished," he said, and with a grinding of stone, the Codex slid back into darkness, its eyes closing. Oliver pushed through the curtains and headed back up the hall. The ritual was easy, except for the VanMuren's Mortar. It was probably something he could get from Dead Désirée. His side ached at the thought. Going to see her was never pleasant. Then again, this would be a good excuse to ask her why she'd given him the portal vision.

Oliver descended the spiral staircase and proceeded down a similar aisle, reaching the curtained entrance for Codex six, where he planned to ask about the Scourge of Selket —

But the curtains were drawn back, the candles extinguished, the stone altar empty.

"I'm sorry," said the Catalog pleasantly from its hidden speaker above, "Codex six has been temporarily removed for information authentication and erudition. Codex six will be returned to service on" — the voice paused as another automated voice, still female but slightly lower in pitch, cut in — "date unavailable." The regular voice returned. "For temporary assistance, please see the librarian."

Oliver stared at the empty chamber. It seemed like too big a coincidence that the Codex containing information about the Scourge would be unavailable at exactly the time when the Scourge had reappeared. Oliver headed back up the stairs, wondering as he went if this was the Half-Light Consortium or Central Council, or both, trying to keep people in the dark until they could solve the problem. Oliver wondered if there was a way to ask his dad about this without unraveling any of the other lies that had brought him to the library in the first place.

Speaking of which, Oliver now arrived outside the curtains marked thirty-four.

"Enter," said the Catalog.

Oliver entered an identical candlelit chamber. He sat on the single pillow and uttered: "Orani."

Orange eyes lit in the dark and the stone pedestal rumbled forward. The crimson-robed Codex breathed heavily, but with less labor than the previous one had. "Continue," it said in a raspy female voice.

"General history," said Oliver.

The Codex inhaled deeply, echoing in the chamber. "The Orani, Overview, as described by Professor Irving Emerick, Sitting High Doctor of the History and Epidemiology of Demo-sapien Bloodlines, Avernus Academy, Morosia: A human tribe cursed with extra-dimensional intuition, the Orani first appeared in

Mesopotamia in the Bronze Age and were worshipped as goddesses. When their fame spread, they were invited to the high court of Pharoah Amenemhet I. Their leaders were promptly enslaved and their followers massacred. But the Orani organized a revolt and disappeared. They have since lived a secretive existence.

"Leaders have often searched for the Orani, seeking their intuitive powers to advise their rule. Emperor Dometian of the Roman Empire and Mehmed II of the Ottoman Empire were reportedly successful in finding an Orani, yet soon after, both of these leaders coincidentally fell ill with conditions of paranoia and insanity consistent with Orani dream manipulation.

"No cited references for the Orani appear after the year 1657, yet they are believed to exist in hiding, and persons of power and influence are still known to seek them." The Codex inhaled again. "Please specify topic to continue."

Oliver hadn't planned on asking else, but something about what he'd just heard struck him, so he said, "Orani dream manipulation."

The Codex inhaled. "Professor Emerick has asserted that Orani can travel into the dreams of another and memories of another to change them. These alterations can lead the victim to believe falsehoods and be consumed by paranoia, guilt, and fear. Emerick theorizes that the Orani are to blame for the mass hysteria that destroyed Arcana in 1868. Please specify topic to continue."

"Finished," Oliver said blankly. He exited, lost in thought about Emalie. He'd had that dream where she seemed to be moving things around, directing the action. She'd been telling him he'd killed Dean, even when he protested that he didn't. It had almost seemed like she was *making* him responsible for Dean's death in his own mind. Was that possible? *She thinks I killed her cousin,* Oliver thought. *Is it so crazy to think that she's after revenge? Maybe she tried to change my memories — maybe it didn't work, or it's taking too long — so she's trying to kill me with sunlight instead.* Could she really hate him so much that she was trying to kill him in two different ways? Maybe he should just try to ask her. *She called me a monster,* he reminded himself sadly. *What good is asking her going to do?*

Oliver reached the final Codex chamber: twenty-two. His brain felt full, and he wondered, with what he'd just learned about Emalie, if he could handle any more worrisome information. He could feel his stomach churning with anxiety. But he was here, and more information on Nexia would be good, because in between thoughts about Scourges and Emalie and Dean's master, there was that rather large question of what Illisius had said, of what it meant to open Nexia's Gate, and why he had to be made different to do it —

He reached for the curtains.

"Occupied," the Catalog informed Oliver.

Oliver stepped back. He checked his watch: They'd been here for half an hour. Bane was probably sick of waiting, and if they were home late for dinner there might be too many questions from Phlox and Sebastian as to what Oliver had been researching. He turned to go.

"Occupant finishing," the Catalog said. Oliver paused and turned back to the curtains. Maybe he did have time if he was quick. The curtains swept open —

Bane stepped out.

For the slightest moment, Oliver and Bane locked wide eyes, and Oliver saw a look of complete surprise on Bane's face. There was no sneer there, no anger in his eyes, just a look that Oliver had never seen before. Did Bane look a little shaken? What had he asked the Codex?

Bane's face changed in an instant, clenching into a menacing frown. His arms shot out and shoved Oliver. "What, are you following me now?"

Oliver toppled backward through the curtains of another Codex. He gathered himself and stepped out of the chamber to find Bane storming down the hall, his boots cracking on the floor.

"Hey!" Oliver called, rushing to catch up. He reached Bane at the elevator. His headphones were already back on. "What were you just doing?" Oliver hissed at him.

Bane glanced at him but just bobbed to his music like Oliver wasn't there.

"What were you doing in there?" Oliver asked as they crossed the loading dock, but Bane remained silent for the rest of the night.

CHAPTER 7

In the Cafeteria

After a day spent tossing and turning over unanswered questions, Oliver met up with Dean on the way to school the next evening. He explained about the master location rite.

"That's great!" Dean smiled. "When can we try?"

"Well, we have to get a few supplies. We need something from Désirée."

"Oh, boy," Dean murmured, "her again."

"Yeah . . . I'm not sure when we can go. My mom's still worried about me going anywhere alone. We'll get there soon, though," Oliver assured Dean.

"All right. Thanks for finding out that stuff."

Oliver looked up to see Dean smiling and looked away quickly. *Just get it over with!* Oliver thought. He needed to tell Dean that everyone thought it was Oliver who was responsible for killing him and then raising him as a zombie. But now he realized why he wasn't: He didn't want to ruin his friendship with Dean. The thought that he and Dean would end up as friends would have sounded funny to him a couple months ago, but now Dean seemed like the only person Oliver could be himself around. Dean wasn't expecting him to be someone he wasn't. *Though he probably doesn't expect you to be his killer.* True, there was that.

"That should be our reason to go see Emalie," Dean continued optimistically, "don't you think? She could help with finding my master."

"Well . . ." Oliver wasn't sure what to say about that.

"I know you're worried she's involved in the sunlight slayings, but if it's putting her in danger, you seem like the best person to stop her. I mean, she might be mad at vampires for killing me, but you're proof that vampires aren't all bad, right?"

"We'll see," Oliver mumbled. "You know, she's probably not even the one doing it. Maybe it was just a coincidence she was at the park." *Because how would she really have time,* Oliver thought, *when she's already busy trying to make me insane?* Oliver had been thinking more about that strange dream. Where had Emalie learned how to enter dreams when she didn't even know she was an Orani? Maybe Oliver had just created that dream. Maybe his brain was being crazy all on its own.

"It would be good to see her," Dean said thoughtfully. "So, any info on the Scourge?"

"Oh, right." Oliver was relieved to be talking about something else. "Nothing. Get this, the information was missing. I think the Half-Light Consortium — that's where my dad works — I think they took it so that the rest of town can't find out what's going on."

"Huh. So that means they're pretty worried about it."

"Yeah." A thought occurred to Oliver. "Dean, if you have a chance tonight, maybe check in on Emalie and just make sure she's home in bed?"

"Oh, can't do it," Dean replied. "I got homeschool tonight. My mom found another zombie kid, named Autumn, and then a human kid named Sledge who's been kicked out of, like, every school in Seattle. Anyway, Autumn's mom is homeschooling us. She's a zombie, too, and studying to be a shaman. She totally keeps us in line."

They'd reached the edge of the school yard. "All right, well, we should check on her soon," said Oliver.

"Cool. Later." Dean headed off into the night.

Inside, Oliver found Theo standing in the classroom doorway. "Nocturne!" he called while simultaneously sticking out his foot and tripping little Berthold Welch as he tried to duck by into class. "Tie your shoes, Welch." Theo grinned.

"Hey, Theo," Oliver said as he walked by, still expecting the same tripping treatment as the other unpopular kids, but instead he got a too-strong pat on the back.

"Dude," was all Theo said. He was grinning from ear to ear.

Oliver was just about to go to his desk when he started to notice the hush in the room, the slight snickers that were escaping from the corners. *What now?* he wondered gloomily. He reached his seat. The snickers twisted into giggles. Oliver looked down —

There was a dead animal on his desk. It was a small brown rat, freshly killed, its eyes still glistening. Oliver knew what it meant at once: the unnaturally twisted head, the red smear on the fur around the neck — it was a valentine.

There was a tiny red bow tied around one of the hind legs, with a scrap of paper attached. Trying to keep his cool, yet feeling the eyes of the room on him, he flipped up the paper. Delicate script handwriting read:

> *How short would be forever,*
> *if we were together?*

A faint scent wafted from the animal, that of its killer. . . . With his stomach lurching queasily, Oliver glanced across the room to see Monique peering out from her clique of friends — and they exploded into laughter.

Oliver burned. The worst part was that this wasn't a joke. This girl whom he'd barely even spoken to had marked him as her valentine — why? Why did this have to happen?

It only got worse at lunch. Oliver tried to avoid it: He made sure he was at the back of the line for his tray of strawberry shortcake. Then he lingered as long as possible at the blood variety machine, before finally deciding on raccoon. He even visited the snack cart, getting a package of gummified centipedes. He finally headed toward the tables —

"Nocturne!" Theo called from nearby. "Sit!" Oliver reluctantly slid into a seat beside Maggots, at the end of Theo's group.

He looked up to see Theo staring at his plate like he was trying desperately not to laugh. "What?" Theo just shook his head. "C-come on," Oliver stammered. "What?"

"Switch!" Theo shouted, and all the boys instantly stood up from the table.

"What are you —" Oliver began, but then, across the room, he saw Suzyn, Monique, and their friends doing the same. "Wait, Theo, no —" Oliver scrambled to pick up his tray, but his centipedes scattered. He grabbed at them and was just standing up, when a cool hand fell on his shoulder.

"Oliver," a confident voice said. He looked up to see Suzyn sliding into the seat across from him. She was almost a foot taller than him, with long, straight black hair. "Sit," she said with a devious smile. Oliver wondered briefly if those were the first two words she'd ever actually said to him. Another girl, Kym, was sitting down beside her. And then Oliver sensed someone sitting next to him. He turned to find Monique. She only glanced at him for an instant, then looked shyly down at her tray.

"So," Suzyn continued importantly, "we've been talking . . ." She said it with so much weight to her words that Oliver thought he might be crushed. "And we've decided that if neither of you are going to make the first move, we will."

Suzyn was smiling devilishly. Oliver just stared at her.

"Oliver," Suzyn nagged, sounding frighteningly like his mother, "you haven't thanked Monique for her thoughtful valentine."

"Oh," Oliver stammered, "oh, right. Thanks," he mumbled, barely getting the word out.

"Monique," Suzyn instructed, "your turn."

"You're welcome," Monique said with a mouse-quiet voice.

Oliver risked a glance at her again and found her eyeing him halfway as well. She flashed an apologetic smile. Maybe she was as sick about all this as he was. . . .

"So it's settled. You two are valentines," Suzyn

continued. "And now, Oliver, I'd like to invite you to my Valentine's Day party this weekend."

"Huh?" Oliver said. He'd lost the ability to use words.

Suzyn went on anyway. "But in order to come to the party, you have to bring a date."

It was like she was an enormous spider, wrapping him up slowly. "O-okay," he said. Across the room, Theo and his buddies watched with wide smiles.

"So, who will your date be?" Suzyn was still staring at him expectantly.

"Um, Monique?"

"Duh . . ." Suzyn rolled her eyes. "So you need to ask her to be your valentine."

"Now?" Oliver gasped. He thought he might turn to dust.

Suzyn nodded.

Oliver felt hot all over. Even his amulet wound was starting to ache. *Just get it over with,* he told himself. He looked over to Monique, his vision swimming with dizziness. Pain shot up and down his side. "Monique," he began miserably, "will you be my . . . valentine?"

There was an explosion of laughter from across the room.

Monique didn't answer. She was still looking down at her tray. Oliver waited. His side was absolutely burning.

Monique didn't look up; in fact, her eyes were closed. Maybe she hated this as much as he did. Maybe they could just be friends, and band together against Suzyn. . . .

Kym huffed, "Monique, come *on*."

Through the din of the cafeteria, Oliver heard a very slight sound. He realized it was coming from Monique. He was the only one close enough to hear it. Was she moaning? "Monique?" He reached forward and touched her shoulder.

"Nice!" Theo called from across the room.

Monique flinched sharply, her entire body convulsing. Her eyes snapped open —

Beams of sunlight sprayed across the cafeteria.

There was screaming, diving to the ground, trays and food flying in chaos. Monique lurched to her feet. Oliver threw himself off his chair as her head thrashed in his direction, the beams of sunlight scalding his forearm as he raised it in defense and setting his shirt on fire.

Oliver hit the ground and his side screamed with so much pain that he wasn't even sure he could move. He managed to claw his way under the table. From here he could see other students ducking for cover, Berthold with his pants smoldering, Theo with slashes of burn across his face. Suzyn was lying on her back in front of him, not moving, smoke trailing up from her. Oliver watched the tender trails of smoke as they rose in the chaos —

And for only a moment, he found himself staring at one of the tiny windows high on the cafeteria wall. It was level with the pavement of the playground outside. There was a figure there, wrapped in a clutching black mist. Despite the eyes shut tight and the brow furrowed in concentration, Oliver knew the face.

Emalie. Her hands were clenched together in front of her, fingers interlocked, with sunlight escaping from the gaps. Her mouth was tight, her face deep in concentration, because she was making the Scourge . . . again.

"Oliver!" He glanced back over his shoulder to see Seth edging along the wall toward the doors. "Get out of there!"

Oliver felt a rush of heat. The table burst into flames above him. Chunks of burning wood rained down. He dragged himself toward Suzyn, daring to look up at the window again —

Emalie was gone.

Oliver fell forward on his stomach. The pain from his side was overwhelming. It was like his legs and his left arm no longer even worked. With all his strength, he pushed himself up on his right elbow and flopped onto his back.

On the other side of the collapsed table was the faint outline of Monique, within an orb of pulsating sunlight. Wind whipped around the room. Oliver felt the heat on his face.

"Uhh," Suzyn moaned from beside him. Oliver tried to reach toward her but fell back. He stared at the charred ceiling. This was it. Emalie had gotten her wish. Oliver felt the fire spreading on his clothes. He was practically blinded by the extreme light in the room —

All at once, it winked out. Monique was gone. There was the faintest sound of ash raining down on the floor.

Some darkness returned, but there were fires glowing everywhere.

"Don't move," a gravelly voice murmured. Oliver looked up to see Mr. VanWick beside him, his coat balled in his hands. He stamped out the fires on Oliver, then picked him up. Oliver noticed another teacher, Ms. Estreylla, lifting Suzyn.

He heard the moans and murmurs of classmates as they were rushed upstairs. Oliver felt cool tile as he was laid down in the first-floor hallway. The green blindness in his eyes slowly gave way to grotesqua dancing above him.

He heard Mr. VanWick nearby, talking with the other teachers. "Call the Consortium. They're going to need a team over here to make this look like a kitchen fire."

"The parents should be on their way already," added Ms. Estreylla.

"Whoever did this may still be outside," Ms. Nikkolai said worriedly.

"Everyone leaves through the sewers," Mr. VanWick added.

Oliver couldn't believe the pain from his amulet wound. It was commanding even more attention than his burns. He tried to sit up and caught a glimpse of maybe ten other students who were lying in the hall with him, their clothes smoldering. A sour smell filled the room.

Oliver laid back, the world blurring. He wasn't sure how much time had passed when he heard Phlox. "Oliver!" She rushed over to him and began lifting him. "Oh, no . . ."

"I'm all right," Oliver said weakly, staggering to his feet.

"Let's get you home." Her voice shook as she moved Oliver's arm across her shoulders.

They started slowly down the hall. Other parents were rushing by to collect their kids. As they passed Mr. VanWick, Phlox leaned toward him. "Thank you," she said. "And don't worry, my husband will find whoever did this."

"Let me know when he does," Mr. Van Wick muttered darkly, his eyes flaring with a lavender glow.

Once again, Oliver felt a wave of worry for Emalie, and yet this time, he almost wondered why. Was it a coincidence that for the second time, someone standing right beside him had been slain by the Scourge? There was no way. Despite how much he wanted to believe otherwise — *What about when she gave you that clipping about your parents?* — what explanation was there other than that Emalie was trying to kill him? And now she was being hunted, and the hunters wanted more than blood, they wanted vengeance. When Oliver wondered what he wanted, he found that he had no idea.

❋

When they arrived home, Phlox escorted Oliver to the couch, and busied over him, tending to his burns. She had to cut his button-down shirt away from his right forearm, where the fabric had gotten stuck to the burned skin. She spread Poultice of Puffer Fish over the blackened, still-steaming area. The burns on his legs weren't as bad and needed only a Cream of Curare and Peppermint leaves, and then thick bandages. By some stroke of luck, Oliver didn't have any serious burns on his torso, and so had been able to keep his T-shirt on, the aching amulet wound hidden. When she was out of the room, Oliver pulled a throw pillow from the couch and placed it across his abdomen as if he was holding it for comfort.

"Okay," Phlox said, rushing back in for perhaps the tenth time. "I'd take you to Dr. Vincent, but I'm sure he's busy with the more serious cases."

"I was lucky." Oliver sighed.

"Lucky," Phlox repeated, her voice thick with worry. "That girl was right beside you, it could have been . . ." She trailed off, handing him a goblet. It was steaming hot, and Oliver smelled a combination of bear blood, krait venom, and crushed sangre del fuego peppers. The venom was a pain reliever, the hot peppers for relaxation. "Drink it all," Phlox said, "and rest."

Oliver drank, then lay back, but there was little hope of rest. As the pain of his wounds slowly lessened, the amulet wound slowest of all, his thoughts careened about. *Emalie is trying to kill me,* he thought miserably. Ever since that first day of school in January, when he'd found the newspaper clipping she'd left him, he'd assumed that there was still a chance that they could be friends. But something had changed. Human hearts were said to heal over time, but sometimes they could be broken beyond repair. . . .

The hours of the evening passed. Phlox bustled about. Oliver imagined that she'd likely cleaned and reorganized the entire house by the time dawn arrived.

Bane returned home. Oliver heard his boots on the stairs, then crossing the kitchen. He opened his eyes slightly and saw Bane peering into the dark living room.

"You're home," Phlox said with relief.

Bane turned away. "How is he?" Oliver was surprised to hear Bane ask that.

"He'll be fine," Phlox said assuredly.

"All right. I'm going to bed." Bane headed downstairs.

Sometime later, Sebastian peered into the room. Oliver continued his ruse of sleep.

"Did you find them?" he heard Phlox ask quietly.

"No," Sebastian murmured. "But we have a lead. We think it's a human, but whoever it is has some kind of cloaking power. There were barely any scent traces. It's mystical power, but we'll get around it next time."

"What do you mean next time?" Phlox hissed. "Next time a child is turned to dust?"

"No, Phlox, relax . . . we're not going to let any more kids —"

"It's been too many already!" she cried. "I want whoever's doing this to pay."

"They will," Sebastian said quietly. "There's an emergency Council meeting downtown in a couple hours. You should go. It will do you good. For now, let him sleep."

Oliver heard them descending the stairs. Phlox's last words lingered in his mind — *I want whoever's doing this to pay* — and he was surprised by the thought he had next: *Maybe Emalie should pay.* Maybe she'd only given him that article to lower his defenses. *How can I think that?* But he found that he did. He might not have a demon yet, but he was a vampire, and this human girl was trying to turn him to dust. *But it's Emalie.* And yet, with his classmates being slain right in front of him . . . Maybe it was the pain of his wounds talking, but Oliver couldn't keep out the surprisingly dark thoughts: *Maybe I'll find her first, only this time, I really will make my first kill.*

CHAPTER 8

Safe Passage

Oliver awoke the next evening to Phlox informing him that school was canceled for the rest of the week. Once she'd checked his wounds and saw that they were healing normally, he retreated downstairs to find that the same could not be said for the amulet wound. Oliver had to pull at the bandage, and it peeled away from his skin with a slight tearing sound. He winced, watching as a fresh dollop of brown bacterial infection dripped out of the wound and splattered on the stone floor. The red lines on his torso now spidered over his shoulder and almost up to his neck. They had doubled again in a day.

He taped a new bandage on, hearing the door to the sewers open and shut as he did so.

"Look who's here!" Phlox said brightly as Oliver entered the kitchen moments later.

Oliver didn't see anyone. Then Dean popped up from behind the kitchen island. "Hey," he said, frowning. He was holding a handful of dishes, which he carried over to the cabinets.

"I'm just having him unload the dishwasher since you were getting ready," said Phlox nonchalantly, as if such a thing was completely normal for a servant.

Oliver felt a surge of embarrassment. "Dean, you can stop now," he said quietly.

Dean looked uncertainly from Oliver to Phlox. She raised her eyebrows skeptically, but nodded. "What your master says, goes, of course."

"Come on," Oliver said quickly.

Looking relieved, Dean put the stack of dishes on the island.

They retreated to the living room and dropped to the long couch.

"Sorry about that," Oliver muttered to Dean.

"I think your mom thinks you're my master," Dean said, looking at Oliver uncertainly.

"Oh, y-yeah," Oliver said quickly, "she's just confused."

"Why would she think that?" Dean wondered aloud.

Oliver looked for a trace of suspicion on Dean's face, but didn't see one. "I don't know. I'll straighten it out with her later."

"Alrighty." Dean seemed to accept the story. He looked cautiously at Oliver. "So I heard about what happened. Mom let me take the night off, too, to see how you're doing."

"Thanks," said Oliver. "I'm all right. Got a couple burns, but that's it."

Dean glanced toward the kitchen and lowered his voice. "Was it —"

Oliver nodded. "I saw her."

"Oh, man . . ." Dean's brow worked. "But why would she attack places where you were? It's not like she'd *want* to slay you, you know?"

"I —" Oliver's brain raced. "Well, she's used the Scourge in a bunch of other places. Bad luck, I guess. Obviously she hasn't been aiming for me." Oliver shrugged, annoyed with himself for lying again.

"Right." Dean nodded. "So now what?"

"Well, my dad and his people will find her," Oliver said darkly, "and that will be that."

"Hey!" Dean slapped Oliver on the shoulder. "What are you talking about? We need to stop her before she gets killed!"

"Why?" Oliver sulked.

"'Cause she's Emalie! What's going on with you?"

"Well . . ." Oliver didn't know what to say. Again, if he said that he thought she really was trying to kill him, Dean would want to know why. *Just tell him.* Oliver cursed himself inside. This issue of whether he'd killed

Dean was just like when Emalie had been visiting his house back in December. Oliver hadn't told his parents, and then enough time went by that the fact that he hadn't told them was just as bad as what he would have been telling them in the first place. And now, Dean might be mad not only that Oliver was believed to have killed him but also that he'd been keeping this from Dean and not trusting him. But so what if Dean got mad for a while? He'd get over it. *But I need him now.* Why? *Because I actually do want to stop Emalie before she gets killed.*

There was that troubling thought. Despite her attempts to kill him, it was true: Oliver wanted to stop her, wanted to hang on to that last shred of hope that they could be friends again. It was easier to remember that when Dean was around, since they had Emalie in common.

"No, nothing," Oliver said. "Fine. You're right, we have to tell her. We should probably go find her now —"

"Oliver." Phlox stuck her head into the room. "I'm heading to the Underground and I want you to come with me."

"Why can't I just stay here?"

"Because I want you with me, considering what's out there. Your father agrees."

"But," Oliver protested, "wouldn't I be safer here?"

Phlox's eyes narrowed. "You're safer where I can see and protect you."

Oliver could see an argument here, but he could also see in Phlox's eyes that it wasn't one worth fighting. "Fine," he grumbled, "just a sec." Once Phlox left the room, Oliver turned back to Dean. "Well, at least I might have a chance to get the Mortar from Désirée. You go find Emalie and keep an eye on her."

"Should I tell her what's up?"

"No — wait till I get there."

"How are you going to get away from your mom?"

Oliver had no idea. "I'll think of something," he said, trying to sound on top of things.

"Roger," said Dean, and hopped up to go.

"Dean," Oliver added, "her house is the only place she's safe. No uninvited vampires can get in. If she tries to leave, you have to stop her."

"How am I going to do that?" Dean thought for a second. "Oh, you mean like knock her out or something?"

"Yeah." Oliver nodded. "But gently. Remember, you have superhuman strength now."

"Got it." Dean ducked out of the room.

As Oliver gingerly got to his feet, he heard Phlox from the other room: "Dean, can you just give the floor a quick sweep after Oliver and I leave —"

"Mom!" Oliver shouted. "Let him go already!"

"All right, some other time, then."

Oliver reached the doorway and saw Dean looking dejectedly back at him. Oliver just shook his head dismissively.

"Come on, honey." Phlox flashed by him, slipping on a long white wool coat and hurrying down the stairs. Oliver followed slowly, grabbing his sweatshirt from a set of hooks on the wall, feeling freshly annoyed. This whole rushing around thing was just how Phlox always got when she was worried and stressed. It was like she'd forgotten that she wanted him to rest.

"What's the hurry?" he said grumpily, his side aching, trailing a few paces behind Phlox as they weaved through the tunnels.

Phlox turned, and her eyes were already glowing turquoise. "The hurry," she snapped, "is so that we're not caught off guard by someone trying to turn you to dust."

Oliver rolled his eyes. What was up with parents sometimes?

The tunnels were busy with vampires, many shepherding their children with them. Giggling and horseplay echoed as kids crawled around the walls and ceiling. Oliver noticed overwhelmed looks on many parents' faces. They were probably second-guessing their decision to shut down the schools right about now.

Oliver also noticed burly vampires at the tunnel inter-sections. He'd never seen security down here before. Outside the double doors into the Underground stood four black-coated vampire guards, watching the pass-ersby carefully.

As they crossed the top, ringed level of the Underground Center, Oliver lagged behind. All this security had given him a thought.

Phlox glanced back, annoyed at his pace, and he made a show of grabbing his arm. Her face softened. "Your burns?"

"They're making me feel weak," Oliver moaned. "Can't I just sit down or something?"

They were right by the food court. Oliver watched as Phlox surveyed the area, which was literally crawling with guards: They were on the walls and ceiling as well as among the tables.

"Well," hummed Phlox, "fine." She dipped into her handbag, then dropped a few *myna* in Oliver's hand. "Get something and *don't leave*. My errands won't take too long. I'll meet you right back here."

"Thanks." Oliver added a pleasant smile. He started toward All Things Rodent, then turned to watch Phlox disappear into the crowd. After a minute, he took off toward the nearest levitation gap. A stop at Désirée's shouldn't take him long —

"Oliver!" He spun to see Dean running toward him through the crowd.

"What are you doing here?" Oliver hissed.

"It's Emalie," Dean panted.

Oliver felt a surge of worry. "Did they find her?"

"No." Dean leaned close and his voice dropped to a whisper: "She's *here*."

"What? What do you mean *here*?"

"I mean here, in the Underground, right now."

"But —"

"I know," said Dean. "I know, but I couldn't do it! She was walking out the basement door, and I was right there ready to, you know"— Dean made an awkward chopping motion with his arm —"but I flinched, and then it was like I lost sight of her."

"How could you lose sight of her?"

Dean shrugged. "She's using something, some kind of dark cloud. I could barely keep track of her, and it's like on the elevators nobody even knew she was there."

"What elevators?"

"Those express ones, you know, down to the charion trains."

Oliver couldn't believe what he was hearing. "Did she get on a train?"

"No, she kept going past them, back into those caverns down there, and then, well, then I came to find you, because I think — I think she's going into the Yomi."

"The Yomi?" Oliver said slowly. Was it possible that Emalie could be that crazy? "Come on," he said, and rushed to the gap. He reached the wall and looked back to find Dean standing at the edge of the level.

"Over here!" Oliver hissed.

"Why? I can just jump down," Dean said proudly.

"No, Dean —" But then Oliver watched a woman callously bump into Dean. He was jostled to the side, where he brushed against a young girl walking beside her father.

"Gross!" the girl whined, and the dad pushed Dean away. His face fell.

"You know what," said Oliver, "go for it." Why should he be embarrassed for Dean? It was ridiculous how these other vampires were acting.

The unsure look on Dean's face remained, but he half-smiled at Oliver's words, then leaped off the edge. Oliver watched him sail downward and land with an awkward stumble on the next level down, setting off frustrated rumblings among the vampires. Without Dean to carry, Oliver took a steadying breath and dropped off the ledge, too. He followed Dean and his wake of annoyed vampires, lowering level by level down to the ninth, where brightly lit tunnels led to the charion station.

"Down here," said Oliver. He crossed to the edge of the level and stepped up onto the railing. Dean joined him and peered down into the dark chasm. "See that ledge over there?" Oliver pointed diagonally across the space, beyond the waterfall and the billowing steam clouds, to a barely visible cavern. "Can you make it?"

"Sure," Dean said, but he didn't sound quite convinced.

Oliver launched himself off the railing, arcing through the steam. It was a long jump for him, but he just made it, then turned to see Dean hit the ledge with his shins and tumble forward, landing on his back on the wet rock. Oliver almost laughed, but Dean was wincing and rubbing his knees. "I'm fine," he said through gritted teeth before Oliver could ask.

Oliver started back into the cavern. They walked through darkness, and then joined a smooth passageway lit with a red tube of magmalight along one wall. The tunnel sloped steadily downward. A gust of wind kicked up in their faces, and they heard the rumble of an arriving charion somewhere behind them. The walls shook.

After a few moments, other sounds penetrated the silence: There was a din like a great many people heard from a distance, the rumble of barely definable drums, and the whining of laboring machinery. The slope of the tunnel increased, then opened up on a vast black space.

"This is as far as I followed her," said Dean.

The floor became a staircase, switching back and forth down a precipitous wall of damp rock. Oliver could vaguely make out enormous stalactites in the shadowy cavern around them. Magmalight lamps dangled down on chains from the unseen ceiling. And there was light from below, but it was out of sight, almost beneath the wall they were descending.

Below, the path turned and tunneled back into the wall. The temperature had grown cooler, the air more damp. The tunnel's ceiling began to rise. Oliver stopped and pointed down. Carved into the floor was a large Skrit:

He looked warily at it. He'd never been in the Yomi. The curved bottom of the symbol indicated that the Yomi was a borderland, sharing a boundary with other worlds that weren't solid. Physical laws could be tricky here.

Oliver had no idea how Emalie planned on surviving this. Sure, she may have found some way to enchant herself so that she was hard for vampires and zombies to see — though Oliver didn't understand how she'd know how to do that, either — but enchantments weren't going to work in the Yomi, not with the physical anomalies. Any spell that even an advanced Orani knew wouldn't be enough.

"Any sign of her yet?" Dean asked.

Oliver checked the air. "Nothing."

"Why do you think she's coming down here?" Dean asked.

"Maybe she needs something to use the Scourge," Oliver mused. "Some ingredient that you can't get anywhere above this."

A shrieking scream echoed in the dark. Oliver had no idea what it was. "All right . . ." he said with a flutter of uncertainty, and stepped forward.

As he crossed the giant Skrit on the floor, the world seemed to shiver and quake, as if he were passing through something more liquid than air — then he was through it. Turning, he saw that Dean was on the other side of a rippling barrier. He stepped through, looking blurry for a moment before emerging beside Oliver.

"What was that?" Dean asked.

"Dead detector. To keep out any living creatures."

"So how did Emalie get through that?"

Oliver just shrugged.

The passage was dark and dank, only now the sounds of voices, machinery, and drums were much louder, washing over them in chaotic swells. Oliver's nose was overwhelmed by pungent odors of warmth, death, and

< 109 >

oil and gas fumes. They walked another minute in darkness, and then emerged from the tunnel into a passageway reminiscent of an alley. Its ceiling reached up into vast darkness. Rickety shops were clustered together on both sides, looming over the path. Some of the shops were just stands; others had windows lit by neon signs in Skrit and other pictorial languages Oliver didn't know.

Billows of steam and smoke washed over the crowd. Above, wooden ladders zigzagged back and forth along precarious bamboo scaffolding that climbed up into the darkness. Some of the ladders led to ledges, some to other stores high up, and some to recesses that were merely dark, gaping suggestions.

There were masses of creatures clogging the corridor, hanging over counters and out of stalls, and lurking in the scaffolding above. Each one seemed hunched or huddled to hide its appearance, sometimes with a hood: Oliver smelled zombies and vampires, and other things unfamiliar, likely true demons who were taking form briefly in the borderland.

The shop owners in the Yomi were Merchynts. They were known as omni-realm demons because they existed simultaneously in multiple worlds. Since it was built in a borderland, this Yomi would also exist in the other nearby worlds, and so each Merchynt would be operating his business in all the worlds at once, appearing different in each.

The only light in the Yomi was from fire: Open metal troughs like gutters had been cobbled together from the roof of one shop to the next, holding channels of continuous flame. Oliver's nose was overwhelmed by the scent of petroleum, being pumped from deep in the earth by those laboring machines. Sometimes the gutters were spaced by a metal bowl, which pooled the petroleum and allowed for a brighter light, but for most of the business being conducted in the Yomi, light was not especially welcome.

"Dude," Dean said nervously, reminiscent of his living self.

"Let's just stay together and move fast." Oliver started ahead, jostling among the secretive figures, keeping his head low among the grunts and hisses. Strange lights glowed in the shops, from signs, from crystal objects, from within the hands of hooded Merchynts. There were displays that looked ordinary at first, like a rack of skinned animals the size of cats — but cats didn't have six legs or only a single eye.

Figures pressed close around and above them. Oliver had trouble focusing and keeping track of direction. Suddenly they found themselves in a gap in the crowd. Glancing about, Oliver saw that everyone had moved into the shadows of the shops. Oliver wondered why —

Until the entire world went black.

It was as if reality had momentarily cut out. The fires were extinguished, the noise of machinery gone — afterward, Oliver couldn't remember if he'd been able to see or sense anything in that single moment — and then they suddenly found themselves standing straight out sideways. The Yomi had turned itself, and now the floor had become the wall. They weren't falling, though. Their feet were rooted to the floor as if "up" and "down" were sideways now, too. A faint red light lit the Yomi.

"What just —" Dean began, but he was drowned out by the deafening blast of an air horn. There was an incredible roaring and grinding of machinery. The ground stayed sideways where it was, but now all the shops, the scaffolding, and the gutters began bending and hinging at millions of joints, rearranging themselves. The shops spun so that they were floor-to-roof, one above the next. Ladders arranged themselves downward from one shop to the next. The gutters made tight zigzags down the shops. Now the Yomi looked like it had been built on the side of a cliff wall.

A hissing sound heralded the arrival of fresh petroleum, rushing downward, splashing carelessly at the zigzagging corners, then igniting with a great sucking of air. Light returned to the Yomi. Oliver could see that everyone around them was quickly taking a firm hold of the nearest ladder.

"Dean, grab my arm," Oliver said, sensing what was about to happen, holding out his hand as he stepped toward a ladder.

"Why —"

A second air horn exploded, and gravity reasserted itself. "Down" became down again, and Oliver's and Dean's feet slipped off the floor. Oliver lunged and was just able to reach a ladder as his body started to fall. Dean managed to grab Oliver's sleeve and swing over to the ladder with a tearing of fabric, and a burst of pain in Oliver's side. He looked up from below. "Sorry."

Everyone in the Yomi began moving again, scaling up and down the ladders. Oliver and Dean continued down slowly, Oliver favoring his arm and leg. He was nearing where the ladder branched like an inverted Y, splitting into two aisles, when he spied Emalie. He swung to the outside of the ladder. "Dean, stop." Oliver pointed. "There."

Emalie was standing across the way at a shop counter, looking so short beside two looming figures. The cloaked Merchynt behind the counter, his eyes and long teeth glowing a luminescent white, was dealing with a zombie on her right. The figure on her left was enormous, with a black business suit tailored to his four arms. Short horns protruded from his bald head.

Emalie was wearing her cheery green vest, her black sweater underneath. A braid slipped out of her black hat. She stood innocently, patiently, a tapping foot the only sign that she might be nervous about her situation. It hurt Oliver to see her there, in such danger. *No more dangerous than being with you,* she might have said, but it was, so much more so. It also hurt just to see Emalie, to imagine her turning around and being glad to see him across the way, yet knowing that if she really did turn and see him, she might just try to kill him. It occurred to Oliver that this was the clearest he had seen Emalie lately. That black shroud seemed to be missing.

"What is that to her left?" Dean murmured.

"Trolgoth demon, I think," said Oliver. "That thing should be having Emalie for a snack right now —"

And as if on cue, the Trolgoth sniffed at the air. It turned its eyeless, waxlike face down toward Emalie. She didn't seem to notice at all. The demon's four arms reached toward her —

"Hey," Dean said nervously, preparing to jump, "we should —"

Oliver watched, frozen. What should they do? Even if they went leaping to her rescue, they were no match for a Trolgoth demon —

A high-pitched hissing sound froze the Trolgoth in its path, its hands inches from Emalie's thin, unaware throat. Oliver looked up to see a fluid ripple of black streaming down the ladder from above. It spiraled around Emalie, coiling like a snake around her body, then lunged up, ready to strike the demon. What had appeared aboveground as merely a shadow had much clearer details here in the Yomi. Oliver could see the smoky black impression of a face hidden by a veil, of bared teeth, and of small, clawlike hands with long nails.

"It's a wraith," he said slowly.

The Trolgoth demon lifted its hands away, even bowed respectfully toward the wraith, which slid back, then uncoiled itself and hovered just behind Emalie's shoulder. It had a vaguely human form, long and lithe, and looked a bit shorter than Emalie, though it was floating above her head now.

Emalie just stood there, seeming completely oblivious.

"Is it going to attack her?" asked Dean.

"No, it's protecting her," said Oliver. "I — I don't know how she's controlling it, or how she hired it, or —" Oliver shook his head, bewildered. This was more dark power. Not only wielding the Scourge but working with a wraith. How was it possible?

"Is it a ghost or something?" asked Dean.

"Yeah, the spirit of a dead person, trapped in this world, sometimes from a curse, sometimes from its own suffering. It's — they're always different."

"I've never seen one before."

"They're only fully visible in the Underworld and the borderlands. That's why Emalie's had that shadow around her. It's been helping her move around, hiding her scent." Oliver felt like a fool for not having figured that out earlier. But how could he have expected Emalie to be dealing with a wraith?

"Are they powerful?"

"Yeah, but unstable."

Dean peered across the way. "What's she doing now?" Oliver watched as the Merchynt looked down at Emalie. The wraith fluttered behind her, and Oliver saw the Merchynt's wrinkled face checking with the wraith now and again as Emalie spoke. The Merchynt's cloak fluttered, and now a wiry hand appeared and placed a tiny silver flask on the counter. Emalie took the flask. As she stuffed it in her pocket, the Merchynt stuck out its hand for payment, but the wraith hissed. The Merchynt nodded.

Emalie stepped away from the counter. Oliver glanced about and saw leering eyes falling on her from all directions. Shadowed figures clambered about to get a hungry view of her movements as she matter-of-factly began climbing up the ladders. Creatures turned and regarded her, but the wraith coiled protectively, hissing and clawing, warding off any wayward arms that couldn't resist reaching for her.

"What now?" Dean asked.

Oliver watched her go. He had no idea. They wouldn't stand a chance against a wraith, not down here, anyway. "We have to wait at least until she's back on the surface."

Just as they started up the ladder, reality blacked out again. When it returned, up and down had shifted again: The wall, which had originally been the floor, had now become the ceiling. The ladder they'd been hanging on to was lying flat beneath them. Oliver and Dean scrambled to stand on top of it. Again, the air horn sounded, and the machinery rumbled. The shops, ladders, and gutters rearranged themselves so that now the Yomi looked like it had been built hanging from a ceiling. The shops were side to side again, with their roofs touching the rock ceiling that had once been the floor. The ladders had become flat catwalks beside the shops, with just enough room to walk without scraping your head. Below the ladders, the scaffolding stretched down into unknowable darkness.

As the hiss of petroleum signaled the relighting of the gutters, Oliver scanned the rearranged world. Emalie was lost from sight. They headed back toward the entrance, but could only move so fast on the bamboo ladders, wary of falling into the abyss.

"We're going to need something to get the wraith out of the way while we talk to her," Dean mused seriously.

"Mmm," Oliver said, deep in thought. *Talking to her, that's funny,* he thought darkly. *She's made a contract with a wraith. A human usually has to sign away their soul or their body or something to get a spirit to work for them. That's how bad she wants revenge on me.* Oliver had to wonder if Emalie could even be talked to anymore.

"So now what?" Dean asked as they passed back through the dead detector.

"Désirée's," Oliver said, turning down the third floor. "Let's get what we need."

CHAPTER 9

Désirée's Wordplay

They pushed through the revolving glass door into the clean and quiet of Désirée's. The store once again seemed empty. The same tinny bossa nova music echoed from speakers in the ceiling. Oliver and Dean walked down the nearest aisle, its perfectly arranged shelves stocked with mysterious tins and jars. They both glanced at their feet as their footsteps made no sound on the tile floor. The scent of bleach lingered in the air, like the place had once again just been cleaned. Oliver squinted, looking ahead through the whitewashed bright toward the high marble counter in the back. It was empty.

Halfway to the back of the store, they crossed a gap in the aisle. Oliver heard a strange, uneven clicking sound and caught a glimpse of movement out of the corner of his eye. Something black and green like the grimy corners and shadows, watching them from the far aisle — but by the time he turned his head, it had flitted out of sight.

"What was that?" Dean whispered.

"I don't know," Oliver replied. He'd had an impression of many arms or legs, of crusted skin, and of eyes that had gleamed gold. Had that been Désirée? *Without her mask?* he wondered.

"Hello, Oliver." Oliver's head snapped back around to find Désirée's tall, thin form standing behind the counter in her pristine white coat. Her back was to them, and she was once again staring into the diamond-shaped mirror in its jade frame on the wall behind her. Oliver shuddered at the sight of her narrow figure, her red hair in a perfect bun, her delicate white hands clasped behind her back. Oliver was struck by that same thought he'd had during their last visit: *That's not what she really is.* He wondered what she saw in that mirror, and craned his neck to see into it, but could only make out the glowing white of what seemed like the reflection of the ceiling lights.

Désirée turned around, a smile stretched across her pristine white face. Behind her thin glasses, Oliver saw no gold gleam, only mild lavender eyes. "It's so nice to see you back so soon," she said pleasantly.

Oliver had been waiting to talk to Désirée again, to maybe even shout at her about the amulet and the vision of his parents, but now, with her smiling pleasantly down at him, he could only get out one innocent word. "Hi," he croaked.

Désirée glanced to Dean, standing beside him, then back to Oliver, her smile unchanging. Her hands appeared, long fingers touching in front of her. "Well," she purred, "I see somebody's been through some changes."

Oliver heard Dean gulp.

Désirée's eyes seemed to narrow one degree as she continued looking at Oliver. "Ah, so many things have changed, haven't they? What happened to your other friend?"

Oliver wanted to blurt out: *You already know.* He could practically feel Désirée picking through his thoughts, learning everything she wanted to.

"I see," Désirée went on. "That's part of why you're here. Well then, first things first. . . ." She reached into her coat pocket and removed a tiny blue glass bottle. She placed it on the counter. "This will help with the pain."

Oliver glanced at it. "What pain?" When he looked back up, he saw the hidden forms of whatever lurked beneath Désirée's mask rolling with enjoyment.

"Oliver . . ." she said, sounding like a teacher. "For your amulet wound . . . Now, ask me."

"What?"

Désirée's grin widened even further. "Ask me the question you want to ask most."

Oliver stared at her and almost felt like he couldn't break from her eyes. He'd imagined himself questioning her before, demanding answers. *Why did you lie to me?* That was always the question he wanted to shout at her. So he opened his mouth and asked:

"Was it real?" The question surprised him, and yet the tremor in his gut that came with it made him realize that yes, this was what he wanted to know most.

Désirée nodded. "Yes, the portal vision was real."

If it was possible to feel both relieved and more freaked out than ever, Oliver did. "B-but how can I believe you?"

"Because you already knew it was real, didn't you?"

"I —"

"Next question."

Oliver could barely keep up. "Wh-why did you give it to me?"

Désirée's face remained smiling. "Obviously because it was what you asked me for."

"But I — I asked you to help me see what that photo showed, and it ended up ruined."

"What the photo would have showed you, it would not have told you what you really wanted to know."

"What do you mean?"

"Oliver." Désirée sounded almost motherly. "You may have wanted to see what the photo showed, but what you really wanted to *know* was what was wrong with you. The photo would have been an answer, but not one that you could have figured out."

"Huh?"

"You are a sired, yet demonless, vampire, Oliver, a truly unique collection of forces and spectra. I don't think your parents, or anyone for that matter, knew exactly what would happen if you were photographed. I think they worried that you might see something disturbing."

"Well, like what?"

"We can't be sure. Without a demon, my hunch was that the photo would have shown you as a corpse, possibly even as an infant, from the night you died. That would have been disturbing for you, and you wouldn't have understood what it meant. No one around you would have explained it to you, which is why I decided to . . . assist. The portal was designed to react to the energy in the photo and use it like coordinates. That way you would have context and a complete answer, as opposed to another confusing question."

"But it destroyed the photo." Oliver saw Désirée's point, but he still couldn't help being mistrustful. What if by destroying the photo she was hiding something from him just like everybody else?

"Yes, sorry about that," Désirée continued. "The transfer of energy to the amulet was powerful, and paper is a delicate thing, after all. But please believe me when I say that what you would have seen would have been upsetting, and also not particularly helpful. The portal was the answer you needed. Though I imagine that was disturbing, too."

"I guess." Oliver tried to work through what he was hearing. "So, the amulet . . . that whole story about me needing protection . . . that was a lie."

Désirée suddenly laughed. Three quick bursts erupted from her, sounding at once delighted and dangerous. Her face snapped into a blank, serious stare. "I don't lie, Oliver."

"I — I didn't mean that you —"

"The amulet of Ephyra is a powerful protective artifact, and while I gave it a second purpose by imbuing it with a portal, its original function is working exactly as I intended it to. It's protecting you right now."

Oliver reached down and lightly touched the area above the wound. Pain echoed up his side, and he felt a rush of understanding. "The Scourge," he said slowly. "It hasn't been missing me."

Désirée nodded. "Indeed, you've been attacked directly with the Scourge of Selket twice now and survived both encounters. If it wasn't for that shard of amulet in your side, you'd be very much a scattering of dust right now. I am sorry, though, that it shattered on you. Sometimes I don't know my own strength with portals. That's why I'm giving you this medication, free of charge. It will clean up the infection." Her smile returned, yet Oliver wasn't sure that the face beneath

< 124 >

was sharing it. "And I tell you what, I'll also knock twenty-five percent off that VanMuren's Mortar that you need," Désirée added, even though Oliver hadn't yet mentioned that.

She glanced at Dean again, who perked up at hearing this. "Finding your master . . ." Désirée said, then clicked her tongue on her teeth. Her eyes flashed back to Oliver. "That should be interesting." Désirée changed subjects before Oliver could respond. "And you also need, I gather, something else?"

"Um, yeah. We need to ward off a wraith."

"Mmm, tricky business." She nodded, folding her arms and tapping a finger on her chin. "Well, of course, nothing works forever. Wraiths are powered by grieving souls and, as you can imagine, those just keep on coming. I do believe I have something, though. . . ." She whisked off into the shelves behind her.

Oliver turned to find Dean raising his eyebrows skeptically.

"Here we are." Désirée returned and placed a square block of black stone on the counter. Its center was hollowed out like a bowl. Egyptian hieroglyphics decorated the borders of the depression. "One VanMuren's Mortar, and . . ."

She placed a small tin beside it. Its gleaming metallic surface was painted with a white, circular-bordered Skrit. "Spread this powder in a protective circle to keep the wraith out. Depending on the wraith's strength, this may buy you up to a half hour. After that, well, as the saying goes, beware most those things that are driven by grief."

"Okay." Oliver nodded. "How about —"

"The Scourge?" Désirée smiled. "I'm afraid that everything I had, I already sold to your father and his team for, let me just say, top dollar." Désirée licked her lips as she said this. "Your amulet shard should be sufficient. Now then, I understand you're in a rush, so that will be fifteen *myna*."

Oliver nodded, not surprised to hear Désirée ask for the exact amount Phlox had given him. He handed her the coins. Désirée placed the items in a canvas bag that was a surprisingly friendly pink color. "Looking forward to seeing you again," she said.

"Yeah," Oliver said wearily, feeling like he probably would. He turned toward Dean. "Let's go," he said, but then stopped. When he looked back again, he thought he saw a moment of surprise on Désirée's face.

"Well now," she breathed, "I didn't think you'd get up the nerve. All right, go ahead and ask."

Oliver hesitated, then did: "Do you know anything about Nexia's Gate?"

Désirée beamed at him. Oliver didn't know whether to feel worried or proud. Dean began to fidget, siding with worried. "Oliver," Désirée said warmly. "I *do*. And

I'm flattered that you would ask, but questions about your destiny must be directed to an Oracle. I could be banned from business for indulging in speculation about your future."

"But — you talk about my future all the time," Oliver said.

"Mmm." Désirée smiled coyly. "It's a fine line, I'll admit. But I'm sorry." She put a finger to her lips. "I suppose there is one thing I could tell you. . . ." She leaned forward, almost unnaturally far over the desk, down beside Oliver so that her lips were by his ear. Oliver shivered, feeling her coarse hair against his cheek, as Désirée whispered, "Selene is best heard through the fires that burn cold." She stood up. Oliver stared at her blankly. "Pretty, isn't it?"

"What's that supposed to mean?" asked Oliver.

Désirée shrugged her shoulders slightly, looking amused. "I'm afraid your time's up."

"But —"

"Oliver!" Oliver spun to see Phlox storming down the aisle.

"Bummer," Dean murmured.

Phlox was bearing down on them, her eyes burning turquoise. "I've been at the food court for"— she checked her watch —"almost a half hour! I've searched every table, alerted security, even called your father! Just what —"

"Good evening, Ms. Nocturne," Désirée interrupted smoothly. "Can I help you with anything?"

Phlox was momentarily caught off guard, and Oliver saw embarrassment flash on her face. Phlox did not like to lose her composure in public. "Désirée," she said as calmly as she could manage. Then she adopted a social tone. "I've just come to collect these wayward boys."

Oliver took this moment to push the pink bag against Dean, who luckily understood. He took it and tucked it inside his jacket.

"Ah, yes. Let me just say, though, in their defense, that they've been a pleasure to talk to."

"Well." Phlox glanced back at Oliver, then talked right over his head again. "That's nice. And what did they come in here to bother you about?"

Oliver couldn't help rolling his eyes. He hated when adults did things like this: acting like he wasn't even there and looking to the other adults to rat them out. Of course, he understood why Phlox wasn't asking him: He'd been planning a lie for exactly this question.

"Oh, these industrious young ones were looking for something with which to battle the Scourge," Désirée went on. Oliver wasn't surprised to hear Désirée lying to his mom, and yet he felt a line being drawn: Désirée was on his side more than his parents', if she was on any side at all. Oliver hadn't thought of himself and his parents as being on different sides exactly, but when it came to his destiny, and Emalie, and even Dean, well, it seemed that they were.

Phlox heard this, and her face lost its edge of anger. When she glanced back to Oliver, he was ready with a sheepish look, saying, "We just thought we could help. I mean, Bane gets to."

"Oliver . . ." The light was fading from Phlox's eyes. "It's nice that you want to help, but you know it's too dangerous." She turned back to Désirée, and Oliver noticed that even Phlox sounded a bit uncertain talking to her. "You didn't — give them anything for that, did you?"

"Oh, of course not." Désirée smiled. "I was just telling them the same thing you did. Besides, I'm sold out."

"All right, well." Phlox nodded and seemed to look away from Désiréc as quickly as she could. "Thank you, Désirée. We'll be going."

"Please do come again," Désirée offered, then slid off into the shelves behind the counter.

"Let's go," Phlox muttered with a wave of her arm. She let Oliver and Dean walk ahead, then fell in step right behind them. "You should have told me where you were going."

"Sorry," Oliver said, resisting the urge to point out that maybe it was a little ridiculous for Phlox to think that Oliver had to tell her everything when she and other

adults didn't do the same for him — but this was not
the time.

✳

They returned home and Phlox whipped up lunch for
Oliver and Dean. She seemed to relax as she scooped a
bowl of mint chocolate chip ice cream and filled a goblet from one of the fresh panda blood bags for Oliver.

"Now, Dean," she said, "I have some leftover goat
livers. I already de-blooded them for a sorbet, but the
meat is still there. Oh, and we have some Gila monster
heads you might like."

"Sounds fine," Dean said innocently.

As they ate, Sebastian swept in. He looked exhausted.
"Hey," he said grimly, adding, "Hi there, Dean."

"Hey," Dean said, trying to crack open a Gila skull as
quietly as possible.

Sebastian pulled a roll of papers from his jacket. He
laid them beside Oliver. "For you. I'm sure this makes
your day."

Oliver frowned at it. "Schoolwork? But there's no
school."

"We are not going to let this disruption hinder our
children's education," said Phlox. "All teachers have
arranged homework until school can reopen."

"Great." Oliver sighed.

"Any luck?" Phlox asked Sebastian hopefully.

"Not enough. There was another attack," Sebastian said grimly, "over on Queen Anne."

Whatever calm Phlox had been momentarily feeling drained from her face. "When?"

"Only an hour ago. Leah's getting better at finding trace force signatures, and we actually traced the perpetrator to this part of town . . . but then the trail went cold again."

"How is that possible?" Phlox asked coldly.

"We put in a request for trackers from the Underworld. They'll be here in a few days."

"Well," Phlox continued as brightly as she could, "at least this one didn't happen within a few feet of Ollie."

Sebastian rubbed Oliver's head. "Well . . ."

"What?" Phlox asked.

"There was an injury . . . to Randall."

"Randall?" Phlox gasped. "What about —"

"Bane's fine. Randall will be fine, too. He lost half an arm, but Dr. Vincent is optimistic about a replacement."

"What were they doing there?"

"Actually, Bane says they had tracked the human to that location."

"How is it," Phlox snarled, "that our son is succeeding where your team is failing?"

"He hasn't told me yet. He was in a bit of a rage about Randall's injury and wouldn't say. You know how he is when he's angry, there's no talking to him —"

There was a loud pop, and Oliver felt warm liquid spray his face. He looked up to see Phlox holding the remnants of a blood bag. She had squeezed it so tightly that it had burst. Her clothes and face, as well as the nearby walls, were covered in blood. "Well then, *force* him to!" she screamed, and her eyes burned past turquoise to midnight blue. "What is wrong with you?!"

"Phlox," Sebastian said, "we're doing everything we can — "

"Then DO MORE!" She hurled the empty bag across the room, where it slapped against the wall. "How close does this have to get before you wake up?!"

Sebastian's eyes glowed amber. Oliver watched carefully, not daring to move. Dean was frozen in place as well. After a moment, Sebastian's eyes cooled, and he nodded. "I have to go back out." He looked at Phlox, his face showing nothing. "We'll talk later."

Phlox only nodded, her lips tight. Sebastian left. After a moment, she picked up a towel and began wiping the blood from the counter.

There was a loud crack and Phlox froze in place, raising her eyes to the ceiling. Oliver looked over to see Dean glancing up sheepishly from the Gila head.

"Let's go downstairs," Oliver said quietly. "You can bring that with you."

Dean nodded. Oliver led the way down the spiral staircase to the crypt. They walked over to the side of his coffin. Oliver held his hand out to Dean. "Let me have the bag from Désirée's. I'll hide the stuff until we have a chance to use it."

"When do you think that's going to be?"

Oliver looked at Dean. "No idea." He reached into the bag and removed the bottle Désirée had given him for his wound. He popped off the top and took a swig.

Dean glanced over Oliver's shoulder. "What's with that?" he asked, pointing with his chin.

Oliver turned to find his coffin opening slowly. "Weird," he said, stepping over and putting both hands on the lid to close it —

But the lid pushed forcefully open —

A figure sat up from inside.

"Dah!" Dean shouted.

Oliver jumped back. His eyes went wide. "What —"

Emalie looked at him coldly. "We need to talk."

CHAPTER 10

Getting the Stories Straight

Oliver just stared. Emalie's clothes and face were grimy with coffin soil. Loose strands of hair sprang from beneath her black hat. She returned his gaze with her wide, clear eyes, but they were frigid, her jaw set. Oliver thought he might explode. Was she here to try to kill him again? He didn't even care. He thought he'd feel mad, but was surprised to find that he wasn't. He just wanted to start talking to her, to say he was sorry again about Dean, to find out how she'd been.

She leaned forward and started to swing a leg over the coffin's edge. Dirt scattered on the floor. Oliver reached to hold up the lid.

"Stay back," Emalie warned icily.

Oliver stepped away. He looked at Dean, who was staring at her in shock.

Emalie got down and brushed briefly at her jeans and vest. When she looked up again, she glared at Oliver.

Her mouth quivered like she was about to say something.

She didn't.

Oliver ran through one thing after another. What to say first? He had nothing.

"Hey, Emalie," Dean said softly.

Emalie's eyes seemed rooted on Oliver. She seemed to be staring right through him.

"I, um . . ." Dean stammered.

Emalie still didn't look at him.

"It's all right," Dean continued.

Finally, Emalie broke her gaze with Oliver, and he understood why she'd been holding it. The moment she looked at Dean, her eyes welled with tears.

"Ah, don't do that. It's —" Dean shifted from foot to foot. He put his hands in his pockets, took them out, put them back in. "I'm fine."

Emalie exhaled, almost like a laugh, then blinked back her tears and wiped hard at her eyes. "Hi, Dean," she said, sniffling.

"Hey. So . . ." Dean continued.

"I know," Emalie said. "You're a zombie. I know."

"How?" Oliver asked.

Emalie's eyes stabbed back at him. "Did *you* do it?"

"I — no! We haven't figured out who raised him yet. We're going to, though, we —" Oliver paused. The shock of seeing Emalie was fading, and now some very important questions were busting into his brain. "Wait. Are you here to kill me?"

Emalie narrowed her eyes. "What are you talking about?"

"You —" Oliver felt a twinge of his recent frustration toward her. "You know what I mean." He glanced around the room, but didn't see the wraith in the shadows.

"No." Emalie shook her head. "I don't know what you mean."

"Well, why are you here?" Dean asked.

Emalie frowned. "I think I need your help."

Oliver felt his frustration growing. "Help? Come on, I'm not gonna fall for that."

"Fall for what?" Emalie turned to Dean. "What is he talking about?"

"He just means," Dean began, like he was tiptoeing on eggshells, "with the way you've been trying to kill him lately. You know, with that Scourge thing."

Emalie's brow furrowed. She eyed Oliver, then Dean again, then Oliver. "I haven't been trying to kill you." There was a loud banging from upstairs: the refrigerator slamming open. Emalie glanced at the ceiling. "Can we go somewhere safer?"

"Safer for who?" Oliver countered. "How do I know this isn't a trap?"

"And you'd know about those, wouldn't you?" said Emalie icily.

Oliver glared at her.

"What's that supposed to mean?" Dean asked, the slightest note of suspicion in his voice.

Emalie seemed to be thinking hard. "Nothing. Can we just go? I'll explain when we're at my house."

"How did you even get in here?" Oliver said, crossing his arms. "Oh, wait." He looked around the corners of the crypt again. "Where's your friend?"

"Guh! What are you talking about?" Emalie huffed. "I just walked in through the sewers. Took me a little while to find the right door," she added.

"Oh, yeah, right, you just walked in." Oliver sniffed the air dramatically. Emalie had no scent. "I know it's mostly invisible aboveground, but it's right here, isn't it? Your little guardian wraith . . ." Oliver couldn't help himself. He hadn't expected to feel this way, but he couldn't hold back his frustration. "We're not going to go with you. If you want to slay me, just get it over with right here."

"I'm not trying to kill you!" Emalie spat. "And I don't know what you're talking about and I don't know what a wraith is. God! Maybe I *should* be trying to kill you." She threw a glance at Dean.

"Okay!" Dean suddenly threw up his arms. "That, right there." He pointed at Emalie. "What's *that* look for?"

Emalie looked at Oliver. He looked back. Fine. It was time to get this all out, before Emalie made it sound all wrong. "Listen, Dean," Oliver began slowly, "I don't believe this is true, but *some* people think that —"

"What?" Dean frowned at Oliver. "Is this the part where you finally admit that maybe you killed me?" His face was like stone.

"No! I mean, I didn't kill you. . . ." He was waiting for Emalie to say something sarcastic, but surprisingly, she kept quiet. "I —"

"Come on, Oliver," Dean muttered, "I may be some lowly zombie, but I'm not an idiot. Your parents thinking you're my master? The way you get all quiet about the night I died?"

"But —"

"Whatever. Zombies can go to libraries, too, you know. . . . Well, I actually just went online. I don't . . . I don't really think you're my master, but you still should have told me."

"I know," Oliver admitted. "But I didn't know how. I wanted to find proof first that I didn't kill you, or —"

"Or you were just a wimp," Dean said dejectedly. "Besides, you're a vampire, you might have killed me. But who cares? It doesn't change the fact that I'm dead. And it doesn't change the fact that we're friends. . . . Well, maybe a little . . ."

"Dean, I swear, I didn't kill you —"

"No, he didn't." They both turned to find Emalie's eyes red and overflowing. "I — I killed you."

Oliver and Dean just stared at her. She choked back a sob.

Oliver threw up his hands. "Now what are you talking about?"

"I'm the one," she muttered, "who found him." She waved her hand at Oliver. "I'm the one who talked you into going to his house, Dean, into going into the Underground, even when you didn't want to. I dragged you into all of this. It's my fault that you died."

No one spoke.

Then Dean exploded. "Oh my God!" He glared from Emalie to Oliver and back again. "The two of you are ridiculous. Get over yourselves! I'm the one who died! I'm the one who's a freakin' zombie! Was one of you raised from the dead by who-knows-who?"

"Well," Oliver started, "but —"

"No." He turned to Emalie. "I jumped down that sewer into the Underground. Nobody pushed me. You don't control me." He turned to Oliver. "And you don't, either. But somebody does, so duh! Can we just figure out who already?"

"No," Emalie said, biting her lip. She looked like she was thinking hard.

Dean threw his arms up. "What?"

"Dean, y-you're right," she stammered. "I mean, I'm so sorry. We can find your master, but —" She looked coldly at Oliver. "I need to know first."

"Know what?" asked Dean.

Oliver felt a light click as thoughts found one another and locked together in his head. "She needs to know if I killed you."

Dean huffed. "I already said it doesn't matter who killed me."

Oliver looked back to Emalie, meeting her cold gaze. "It does," he said. Emalie's eyes didn't waver. "If we're ever going to be friends again, it does."

Dean sagged. "I can't believe this. You know what? You two do it." He reached toward Oliver. "Give me the locating stuff. I'll get my mom to help me or something."

"No, Dean," Emalie said, "we need your help —"

"No you don't!" Dean shouted. "This is all about you two! And honestly, you guys never really need my help. All I did was get in the way when I was alive, what's the difference now?"

"Dean, come on," Oliver said, "that's not true."

"Tell me that when I was alive you didn't want me dead, or at least out of the way."

"I —" Oliver began, but Dean was completely right. "I mean, maybe a little, but things have changed. We're friends now."

"Yeah." Dean sighed. "Except when I'm emptying your stupid dishwasher."

"We'll straighten that out, Dean, it's just been crazy!"

"I know, but . . . hello! It's been crazier for me!" He pinched at the dead skin on his forearm as if to point out all he'd gone through, and a piece actually came free. "Guh," Dean groaned, and stormed off.

"You're right," Oliver called after him.

"Yeah I am." Dean left the crypt and leaped down the stairs.

"Dean, wait!" Emalie called. Oliver heard the sewer door creak open, then slam.

Oliver and Emalie were left alone. They both looked anywhere but at each other.

"Bane?" Phlox called down the stairs. "Is that you?"

"Dean left," Oliver called.

"Oh," Phlox said worriedly. "All right."

Oliver waited, thoughts flying around in his head, trying to find some that made sense. Upstairs, Phlox's busy kitchen sounds returned. "How are we going to prove I didn't kill Dean?"

"The same way I've been trying to all month," Emalie explained. "I've traveled into the memories of almost every person who was there that night."

"That's what you were doing in my head," said Oliver.

"Yeah."

"I thought you were trying to drive me crazy. I — I heard that Orani can do that."

Emalie half-laughed, but gazed at him oddly. "You know about that. Me being Orani."

"I — I did some research. I was hoping to tell you sometime —"

"I found my mom's old notebooks," Emalie said, looking at the floor. "She left them with her darkroom stuff. I always thought it was just junk, but I found out a lot about me, or us. Her and me. It's always nice to know there's a reason why you're a freak." She kind of smiled.

"Yeah," Oliver agreed. He felt an amazing gust of relief, as their conversation was becoming more normal, like it used to be.

"There was an enchantment," Emalie continued, "for traveling into people's memories while they're asleep. I know what *I* remember from that night, but I thought, well, I thought it was possible that there was more to it."

Oliver wondered what to say. He had been right. The article, the hope that there was still a chance . . . He felt like saying *thank you,* but kept quiet.

Emalie continued, "I've been into most of the schoolkids' memories, and yours. . . . I can tell there's something there. It's like reality's been changed. Something's messing with all the memories, but whatever it is I can't get around it. Nothing works." She looked up. "I thought you could help. Maybe you or Dean can see something I can't, but —"

Oliver caught the faintest advance smell, and suddenly he lunged at Emalie. "What!" she cried, but Oliver threw a hand over her mouth. In a lightning motion he lifted her up and dumped her into his coffin.

The basement door slammed open. Bane's boots rocketed up the stairs.

Oliver leaned over Emalie, whispering: "Stay in here for a minute, don't make a sound — you have to do this, or he'll kill you."

Emalie's eyes were wide. She had no reason to trust him now — but she nodded.

Oliver shut the lid.

Bane swept into the room. "Hey —" Oliver began, but Bane rushed at him and slammed him in the chest with both hands. Oliver flew across the room and hit the wall. He crumpled to the ground, his side and back screaming. He tried to speak, but his chest was clenched too tight.

"That felt good," Bane hissed. He glared at Oliver, his eyes burning. "I almost had her tonight, bro."

"What are you —"

"Your girlfriend!" Bane shouted. "Your murderer girlfriend. You know she's doing it, don't you?" Bane paced between the coffins.

Oliver slowly stood up, staying against the wall. "How do you know it's her?" he asked.

"I just know," Bane growled. "We watched her go down into the sewers tonight, then we waited for her. Started tracking her the minute she came back to the surface. We followed her to this little park on Queen Anne, and wouldn't you know, she sits down and goes all into this trance. We started toward her and suddenly she's up and firing at us before we could even react."

Bane grabbed Oliver by the shirt and pinned him up on the wall. "Randall lost an *arm*, lamb! And what are you doing about it? Hiding out here at home with Mommy? It's your fault she's out there dusting us! You had to go make friends with her."

Oliver was listening, but he was distracted by the sight, over Bane's shoulder, of Emalie cracking open the coffin lid and peering out.

"What?" Bane dropped Oliver and spun around. The lid was already closed again. He sniffed the air, then turned back to Oliver. "Your little servant's not going to come save you. I saw him leaving."

Oliver sighed inside. Bane hadn't sensed Emalie. And over Bane's shoulder, Oliver saw a faint smoky shadow curling up from behind his coffin. It was barely visible, but Oliver recognized the wraith, protecting Emalie, keeping her scentless.

Bane shoved Oliver again, then turned and headed out. "I'll find her, and it's going to be rad when I do. Maybe I'll bring you home a souvenir." He stormed upstairs.

Oliver shook with anger. He walked back over to the coffin, which was slowly opening again. Emalie looked at Oliver wide-eyed. "What was he talking about? I —"

"Just get out of here," Oliver said coldly. "Go home, where it's safe." He didn't know whether to believe her — the way she seemed to have no clue about the Scourge — but all that mattered right now was that she got out of his house before someone found her. "I'll try to get out after dinner, and I'll meet you in your basement, if — if I'm still invited in." He looked at her uncertainly.

Emalie slid out of the coffin. "You are." She turned for the door. "I'll see you later." She headed quietly down the back stairs, the faintest black shadow trailing her as she went.

Oliver spent the rest of the night at home, restless. He sat in the kitchen and made a show of working on his homework, but got almost none of it done. Bane headed back out a few hours later, ranting about vengeance. Oliver listened worriedly, but Bane didn't mention

Emalie. Oliver wondered why Bane hadn't told Phlox or Sebastian that he knew it was her. Maybe because he wanted to kill her himself.

Oliver ate dinner alone in front of the TV. Phlox was too wound up to sit and eat, and Sebastian wasn't coming home.

He waited another hour after dinner, then told his mom that his wounds still hurt, and that he was just going to go to bed early. He changed into pajamas, walked back upstairs to say good night, then returned to the crypt and changed right back into his clothes and sweatshirt and sneakers. He collected every dirty piece of his clothing that was either around his coffin or in the laundry and piled it in his coffin to keep his scent in the air, then he closed the lid, grabbed the bag from Désirée's out of his dresser, and stole off into the predawn darkness.

CHAPTER 11

Into the Memory

Emalie's house was dark. Oliver approached from the alley. Sunrise was still an hour or two away, but the first birds and alarm clocks were beginning to chirp. He found the back door open and Emalie sitting on the floor in her tiny space among the cardboard boxes, back against the washing machine. A thick pillar candle stood lit beside her, and Emalie was squinting hard at a beat-up spiral notebook.

"Hey," she said as Oliver entered the room.

He hid his surprise, as he'd been moving as quietly as he could. Emalie's work as an Orani had heightened her senses. Oliver crossed the room warily, still the slightest bit unsure of whether another Scourge attack was coming. "Hey." He started to sit down when something hissed beneath him.

"Amey, shush," Emalie said. A tiny tan kitten darted away from Oliver, hiding in the shadows, where its luminescent eyes were joined by a second pair. "Don't mind them," said Emalie, "Amethyst and Jade were my Christmas present from Dad."

Oliver nodded. He wasn't sure what to say so he looked around the room. The string where Emalie had hung photos was empty. "Taken any new pictures?" he asked.

Emalie just huffed lightly. "Camera's ruined."

"Oh. How's your dad?" Oliver asked. "Still the same?"

"No he's not the same," Emalie huffed, glaring at him. "Nothing's the *same*. It's been, like, two months!" She looked back down at the notebook. "But he's a little better. He got a job down at the docks. My great-aunt Kathleen hired him for her salmon-fishing business."

Oliver watched her as she read. "Is that your mom's notebook?"

"Yeah." She flipped it closed. "I've been reading it after Dean . . ." She trailed off.

"How did you know?" Oliver asked carefully. "I mean, that Dean was back?"

Emalie shrugged. "I go to his grave a lot," she said softly. "It's peaceful there. One night I saw the mess after he climbed out. Then I walked up to his little brother at school and just said, really quick: *How's Dean?* And he was like: *Good,* and then he realized what I'd asked and he freaked out. So I watched them through their window one night, and I saw him. I know he's been following me lately. He's not so subtle."

"Yeah," Oliver agreed.

"You've been — good to him," Emalie said quietly.

"I just —"

"I didn't want to see him until I was sure what had happened that night."

"Well, he wanted to come see you right from the start," Oliver admitted. "I told him not to, 'cause I wanted to find out what had happened, too."

"Do you think he'll come around?" Emalie asked.

"Yes," Dean's voice muttered tiredly from the shadows. Emalie and Oliver turned to find Dean trudging into the basement. He dropped to the floor beside Oliver. "Let's just get this over with so we can get on to stuff that matters."

"Hey, Dean," Oliver said.

"Hi," Emalie added.

There was a moment of silence. It felt like each of them was just about to speak —

"God, let's just do this already," Dean groaned.

Emalie nodded and flipped the notebook pages. "My mom found out she was an Orani from her aunt," she offered, like she knew what Oliver was wondering. "It skips around in families. Not everybody is one."

"But you are."

"Yeah." Emalie sighed, "I guess. I got the hang of this memory visiting pretty quickly." Her tone lightened a bit. "It's kinda cool. You put this talisman outside a person's window or nearby somewhere." She held up a large, weathered gray coin. Oliver could see the marks where it had been hammered by hand. In the center was a simple diamond shape, with two dots side by side inside it.

"It's called a memory rite. It works like a door into the person's mind. You use it while they're asleep so that you can be in their heads without them knowing." She put down the coin and produced the small flask that Oliver had watched her buy in the Yomi. "So then you sit near the person's house and rub a drop of this stuff on the inside of each wrist, and then you try to relax, and then, well, then things get weird and you end up inside somebody's head."

"And once you're in there you can find the memories you want?" Oliver asked.

"You have to wander around for a while, but yeah," Emalie continued. "It's not too hard. It's like, you can kind of feel your way to the right memories. And everyone who was in the gym that night has been thinking about it a lot, so the memories are near the surface. I think I might show up in kids' dreams while I'm in there."

"Yeah, I saw you in mine," said Oliver. More pieces were clicking together in his thoughts. "Wait, so were you doing this enchantment earlier tonight?"

"Well, yeah . . ." Emalie said. "I had to get more of this"— she shook the flask —"and then I went over to Ms. Reynolds's house, that's the choral teacher, and I went into her mind, but I didn't find out anything new."

Oliver finally understood. "You leave your body behind when you do this. . . ."

"Yeah," said Emalie. "It's pretty strange . . . I mean, I use this protective circle, made of gypsum sand — that's another thing from Mom's notes — but sometimes when I come out of the person's head, I'm somewhere different than where I started."

"So, you also went into someone's memories on Tuesday night?"

"Um," Emalie said uncertainly, "yeah, I did."

Oliver nodded. It made sense. "You really don't know, do you?"

Emalie's eyes narrowed. "Don't know what?"

Oliver thought out loud. "You didn't hire the wraith . . ."

"Why do you keep saying that?" Emalie griped. "What's a wraith?"

That was it. A wraith wasn't able to possess someone when they were conscious. It could only stay near

Emalie, protecting and concealing her, without her knowing it. But if Emalie was leaving her body . . . "Listen, Emalie, a wraith is a spirit. And while you've been traveling into people's minds, one has been taking over your body."

"What are you talking about?" Emalie sounded angry, or scared, or maybe both.

"Well, you said you end up in different places. . . ." Oliver said carefully. "While you're in a person's head, this wraith is possessing your body and using you to kill vampires. It's using an enchantment called the Scourge of Selket. It slays vampires by infecting them with sunlight."

Emalie just stared at him. "But I'm not —"

"I know. You don't know it's happening. . . ." Oliver felt relief wash over him.

"He thought you were trying to kill him," Dean added.

"Why would you think that?" Emalie said quietly.

"W-well, I didn't really," Oliver stammered. "I mean, I was worried that you were, but since you gave me that newspaper clipping, I didn't really think —"

Suddenly Emalie's face twisted darkly. "Wait, what clipping?"

"The one you left under my desk, about my parents' deaths."

"I never left that under your desk!" said Emalie. "I lost it, or someone stole it. I mean, I copied it at the library, and I was thinking of maybe giving it to you, but then it disappeared."

Oliver felt like he'd been stopped dead in his tracks. *Then who gave it to me?* he wondered. And what did that mean?

"Can we get on with this whole memory thing already?" Dean pouted.

Oliver shook his head. More questions for later, but Dean was right. They had to get on with it. He reached into Désirée's bag and produced the small, square tin. He popped it open, and a coil of red vapor curled out.

"What's that?" Emalie asked.

"It's a powder that will ward off the wraith, at least for a little while."

Emalie looked around. "What wraith? There's nothing here!"

"There is!" Oliver said. "You just can't see it. Look, you have to believe us. *We* saw it protecting you in the Yomi."

Emalie's eyes narrowed. "You were following me in the Yomi?"

"Oh, boy," Dean sighed, smacking his forehead.

"Yeah, didn't you know?" said Oliver.

"No —" Emalie started, sounding annoyed.

"Let's just do the spell," Dean moaned.

"Well, of course we did," Oliver continued. "You were crazy to go down there."

"No I wasn't!" Emalie shouted. "My mom had notes about how to make a protection charm to wear so that nothing would hurt me." Emalie pulled a necklace from her shirt. At the end of a leather strap was a tiny figure, woven from straw. "She said it didn't always work, but it's worked great for me. This is what kept me safe!"

"That?" Oliver almost laughed. "That might have kept you safe from the roaches, but not the demons that were around you —"

"What do you know, Oliver?" Emalie countered. "I made this! I'm an Orani and this keeps me safe. It — it does a better job than you could have done!"

Oliver stopped. He had no idea what to say next. This was all going to fall apart if they kept talking in circles like this. So instead he stood up. "Just watch," he said. He held the tin straight out, then slowly spun in a circle, releasing the powder around them. Instead of falling to the floor, the powder hung in the air, then began to both drip toward the floor and float toward the ceiling, building a transparent, circular wall around them.

Emalie looked around. "So what's that supposed to —"

Suddenly a shrieking hiss tore at their ears. It seemed to be coming from everywhere at once. There was a rush of air, and now something vague and black hurtled down among them. Oliver was knocked back to the ground. The hissing became high-pitched: an inhuman scream. Emalie, Oliver, and Dean braced against a vortex of wind as the blackness gathered shape, becoming a long, undulating form. It spun madly. Oliver felt a rush of cold. He caught the faintest glimpse of teeth, of a face curled in rage, of claws. The scream was deafening —

And then silence. Oliver looked up. The red powder had reached the ceiling and the floor, closing off a circular chamber around them. He peered through the shimmering red. The wraith flashed by, circling the cylinder like a shark. Emalie and Dean gazed out as well.

"That's been using me?" Emalie said quietly. "Okay . . ."

"We have to hurry," Oliver urged. "The powder won't last long."

"And what are we going to do when this protective thingy runs out, I mean, about the wraith?" Dean asked.

Oliver shrugged. "Don't know yet."

Emalie looked at him, and their eyes locked with purpose. She thrust the stone memory rite into his hands. "You hold this." She picked up a jar from beside her, stood, and made a circle of gypsum sand around the three of them. Then she sat back down, cross-legged, and opened the silver flask. She dabbed a drop onto one finger, and rubbed it in small circles against the other wrist. She repeated this, then held out her hands, one palm up and one down. "Like this," she ordered.

"Whose head are we going into?" Oliver asked.

"Yours again," Emalie replied.

Oliver and Dean awkwardly put their hands out. "Come on already," Emalie urged. "Oliver's on Dean's, Dean's on mine, mine on yours." Oliver got his hands into place. "Close your eyes and try to focus just on the hands."

Oliver did so, the memory rite in the palm that Emalie put her hand atop. Focusing was tough because he was worried: What if, after all this, they found a truth he didn't want to know? What if what they were about to see really ruined everything . . . ?

And then there was a rush of darkness and loss, like traveling backward into Oliver's head, away from the edge where his senses were, where the view out his eyes was — back inside, and back to the night.

✦

Oliver found himself in the hallway at school. Dean and Emalie were beside him, Dean a zombie, Emalie in black, as they'd looked in Emalie's basement moments before. The neon grotesqua glowed on the walls, but there was that sunlight that seemed too red streaming in through the windows. And the floor was made of grass.

"My head's a weird place," Oliver muttered.

"Actually, yours is pretty lame compared to a human's," Emalie commented as she headed down the hall. "You wouldn't believe what's on the minds of kids my age. Sheesh."

Dean and Oliver followed her, their eyes meeting for just a second. Oliver thought Dean looked worried. *Maybe for the same reason I am,* Oliver thought. Dean might have said that it didn't matter who killed him, but what if it turned out Oliver really had? How were they going to deal with that?

They reached the double doors into the gymnasium. Emalie pushed through them. Inside, they found everyone from the night of Dean's death standing frozen in place. The kids were huddled together, Bane and his friends Ty and Randall in a triangle surrounding the humans. Oliver glanced off into the dark recesses of the gym. There he was, crouched on the basketball backboard, barely visible. Everything was still, waiting to begin.

"Let's stand over here," Emalie said to Oliver and Dean, pointing to an empty space by the wall. She turned to the frozen scene before them and put out her hands. "Here we go. . . ."

The memory jumped to life.

"Look," Bane called toward the darkness as he had that night, "big brother is here to help, so if you don't come down, here's what I'm going to do: I'm going to kill each of these kids, one at a time, until you do — starting with this one!"

Oliver and Dean watched it happen all over. There was no changing it: Bane making Oliver choose, Emalie mouthing the words *pick me* to try to protect the other terrified kids, and finally Oliver choosing Dean and leaping at him. And all the while, Bane holding that staff with the swirling turquoise orb on top.

In the memory, Oliver slammed into human Dean and tackled him to the floor.

"That hurt," zombie Dean commented. Oliver could tell that he was trying to sound funny, but his voice sounded tense. They were getting close to it now. . . .

"This is the part to watch," Emalie said, holding her hands out against the air.

Oliver noticed that Bane had moved the staff in front of him.

"Ahhh — noo!" human Dean screamed in the memory, Oliver's face by his neck.

Oliver watched carefully as his memory self glanced quickly toward the door. He remembered this, planning to leap free. "Okay," he said quietly to zombie Dean, "this is where it should change, because right here —"

A huge voice thundered through the gym: *"Oliver, don't fight it, my boy. It's time. . . ."*

"Who was that?" Emalie asked.

"That was Illisius," Oliver explained. "He's . . . he's my demon. This is the part where I leave, and he shows me the Gate."

Both Emalie and Dean looked at him, perplexed. "The what?"

"I'll explain later. But watch — I'll leave right here," Oliver said, trying to sound certain. He watched Bane in the memory. *He'll use that staff somehow. Here it comes. . . .*

"Oliver, no!" human Dean screamed from the floor.

Bane didn't move. The staff stayed as it was.

"Ahh!"

Oliver looked down and found that in the memory, he hadn't left. Instead . . . he had sunk his teeth into Dean's neck.

"Ah —" Human Dean's voice was cut off. There was an awful sound of gurgling blood.

"Whoa, okay . . ." zombie Dean mumbled blankly. He didn't sound upset by what he was seeing, but Oliver didn't think that would last much longer.

"Like I said, you do it every time," said Emalie sadly.

"That's not what happens!" Oliver shouted, watching helplessly as he killed Dean. "I wasn't even here!"

"You say that, but this memory is in your head. . . ." Emalie pressed against the air. "Something is weird about it — like something's been changed, but . . . I don't know."

In the memory, Oliver leaped to his feet, wiped at his blood-covered mouth, which was twisted in an evil grin, then turned and ran from the room.

"But —" zombie Dean breathed, watching.

"Nicely done, bro!" Bane called, that staff still unused. "Let's go, fellas." He turned and sauntered back toward the exit. Ty and Randall followed Bane out. As soon as they were gone, the children began screaming and sobbing and running terrified for the exit. In moments, the gym was empty, except for Dean lying lifeless on the floor, and the Emalie in the memory sitting on the risers, face in her hands. Now she dug in her bag, removed her homemade vampire stake, and stumbled out of the gym.

"It — it doesn't make sense," Oliver pleaded. "I *left*." He turned halfway toward zombie Dean. "Dean, I swear —"

"Shut up," Dean said quietly. He didn't sound mad. His brow was furrowed as he peered at his body, like he was trying to understand what he was seeing.

Emalie walked over. Her eyes were red. "Dean —"

He threw up his hand. "Duh!" He pointed emphatically toward his body. "Look!"

Oliver turned toward the body lying alone in the gym.

Emalie looked from the body back to Dean. "Dean, I think you're already dead."

Dean glanced momentarily at Emalie and rolled his eyes. "Not at me, at *him*."

"Who?" Emalie looked back at the lone body, confused, as did Oliver. He felt a swell of guilt. Dean was still trying to see something to disprove what they'd seen. But Oliver had killed Dean. Maybe while in his mind he'd been off with Illisius, his body had acted in its true nature. . . . He'd wanted so hard to believe that Bane had done it. "Dean, I —"

Dean looked up, anger finally in his face. "What is wrong with you?" He pointed back at his body. "Look . . . what's he saying?"

"Dean, he's — I mean, you — aren't saying anything. I think you're already dead," Emalie added sadly.

"I never wanted to kill you," Oliver began.

Suddenly Dean's eyes grew wide. "Oh, I get it." Amazingly, he smiled. "You guys don't see him, do you?"

"Who?" Oliver asked.

Dean nodded. "Wow." He turned to Emalie. "Can we watch the memory again?"

"It won't do any good —"

Dean shook his head. "This time can we see Oliver's memory the way I see it?"

"You're seeing something different?" Emalie asked.

"Duh, yeah." Dean almost laughed.

"Okay." Emalie moved between them. "Um, Oliver, give Dean the memory rite." They made a circle of their arms. Emalie closed her eyes, her face twitching like she was busy. "This is tricky, but all right, here goes. . . ."

There was a blur, and the memory ran in reverse.

"There," Dean said. "From right here."

The memory began again. They were still inside Oliver's head but seeing what Dean saw. It started the same. "Oliver, no!" human Dean screamed from the floor. In the memory, Oliver was on him, just about to jump.

"Oliver, my boy," Illisius began to speak —

But now a blinding flash of turquoise light exploded from the top of Bane's staff. Light washed over the room, radiating out from the orb, freezing everyone in the memory. The entire world around them became lit with cold blue. Everything, even the specks of dust floating in the air, was completely still and glowing softly, as if made of ice. Oliver, Emalie, and Dean stood to the side, gazing at the frozen moment in wonder.

"Whoa . . ." Emalie whispered. "How come you can see this?"

"I don't know, just watch," Dean said with an almost triumphant smirk on his face.

Oliver looked back to Bane, relieved, ready to watch him manipulate events, except Bane wasn't moving yet. In fact, he seemed to be frozen, too.

And then, from the dark recesses of the gym, a figure swept silently across the frozen scene. He was dressed in a deep blue robe, his face hidden by a hood.

"Who's that?" Emalie asked blankly.

"I don't know," breathed Dean, "but I think this is what really happened."

The figure knelt beside the frozen Oliver and Dean. He pulled Oliver off, rolling him onto his back. He put his hand to Dean's neck, holding out his first two fingers. With long, pointed fingernails, he pierced Dean's skin. He gathered blood on his fingers and smeared it on Oliver's face. Then he reached into the folds of his robes and produced a thin silver syringe. He planted the sharp tip in one of the wounds on Dean's neck and depressed the plunger.

"So that's when he kills me," Dean said, like a narrator.

The figure began whispering in Dean's ear, chanting, it sounded like. "This is what I was trying to hear when you guys wouldn't stop talking," Dean explained. "But I still can't get it."

"It's another language," Oliver added, straining to hear the whispers. "Demonic, I think."

"Do you understand it?" Emalie asked.

Oliver shrugged. "No."

The figure took Oliver's frozen body in his arms and stood. He stepped away toward the door, then turned back. He took a deep breath, then started to blow. Air began to rush, washing over the entire room. Then he rushed out with Oliver.

As the wind swirled around the frozen scene, the turquoise faded and the spell was broken. Now everyone started moving. Bane shook his head, then looked quizzically at the turquoise orb. He turned and saw Dean's body lying there, and his confused look became a smile. He called to his friends and they took off. The memory became the same as what Oliver remembered now, the children screaming and fleeing, Emalie upset, then heading out, stake in hand, to find Oliver upstairs.

"I thought it was Bane," Oliver said, "who altered our memories."

"I think he knew that orb would do something," Emalie said. "But that figure was really in control of it. Maybe he's the one Bane got it from. Or maybe Bane never even knew that person controlled the power of the orb."

"My master," Dean said blankly.

Oliver nodded. "Yeah. That's got to be the person who raised you. Not that we know who it was."

"Maybe the enchantment," Emalie mused, "the one that he used to alter everyone's memories, was designed to work on humans and vampires, but not zombies," said Emalie.

"Zombies are supposed to be immune to a lot of that stuff," added Oliver.

Emalie turned to Dean. "I guess it's a good thing you were here."

"Yeah," Dean said, satisfied. "And Oliver didn't kill me."

Oliver looked from Dean to Emalie. "No, I didn't."

"And you didn't, either," Dean said to Emalie.

"Well . . ." she started.

"So now you can both get over it," Dean announced.

Emalie nodded. "We should get out," she said, and started for the door. "We have to go back to that point where we entered Oliver's head, in the hallway, and then I can bring us back."

"Right." Dean patted Oliver on the shoulder. "So . . . cool, huh?"

Oliver smiled. "Yeah, cool. We just have to figure out who your master is."

Dean nodded. "We will."

They pushed through the double doors back into the hallway. Oliver noticed the red light through the windows again. It didn't seem like daylight, more like that of another world.

"Hurry up, Oliver," Emalie called from ahead.

Oliver walked along, then spied a door and stopped. It was simple, solid black wood, with a white diamond-shaped Skrit carved in it. He hadn't noticed it on the way in.

"Oliver!" Emalie called.

But Oliver was grabbing the silver door handle. What was this? The door clicked open. Inside, he saw a small, spare room. There was a desk and a comfortable chair. The side walls were lined with black bookshelves, empty except for a book or two here and there. On the back wall was a large, diamond-shaped window. Through it, Oliver saw the red lands and starry, crystal-black sky of Nexia. There was a pyramid of gleaming jade in the distance. Lying on the red rock, closer, was the head from a huge amethyst statue. It had gold eyes that gleamed like coins. Oliver could barely focus on that, though, because beyond that, overwhelming everything, was the Gate.

As soon as he saw it, Oliver longed to sit down in that comfortable chair and just stare at it. It was enormous, shining in golden light. He felt like he could just make out its form, its towers and columns, but more than that . . .

Oliver, the Gate spoke in his mind, *see me clearly.*

"Oliver!" Emalie's voice was urgent, but distant. He wanted to stay here, maybe read a book or two — because there would be more books, he felt sure of that — and gaze at the Gate. . . .

This is my place in your mind, Illisius's voice echoed in the room.

Suddenly his side exploded in pain. Oliver stumbled backward, out of the room and into the hall. He looked up wildly. The door slammed shut. The grotesqua was gone. The hall had gone black. Its sides were melting away in chaotic ripples.

"Oliver!" It was Dean, but he sounded far away.

Oliver's head scared as the hissing cry of the wraith burst through everything. He looked ahead and saw blackness, and the coiling form looming over him, claws bared —

There was a rushing of light, and hands grabbed him. Oliver looked up to see Dean and the rafters of Emalie's basement. They were out of his head, back in the basement, and Dean was dragging him to his feet.

"Come on!" he shouted.

But Oliver's side felt like it had tied itself in a knot. He couldn't move.

There was another wicked scream. Oliver looked up —

The curtain of red vapor was gone. Emalie stood over him, shrouded in black, her eyes shut. Her hands were clasped together, and burning light as if from a sun radiated between her fingers. They hadn't gotten out in time, and the wraith had possessed Emalie. It shrieked now, and Emalie opened her hands.

The air rippled with heat, and Oliver felt the full power of the Scourge hit him directly. The pain from his side brought spots to his eyes. He flopped to the ground, and now he felt hot, searing fire all over his body. His eyes went white with brightness, and he was vaguely aware of the sunlight escaping from them —

No! he screamed inside, sunlight bursting from his mouth, *The amulet shard isn't enough — I —* He felt burning all over and a terrible panic as the world became light — then everything ceased.

Chapter 12

Removed

"Oliver . . ."

Oliver felt like he was floating to the surface of deep water. *Is this the drift?* he wondered. The drift was where many believed a vampire went after being turned to dust, but he sensed light. . . . His eyes fluttered open and he squinted against brightness — *the Scourge!* — but it was the moon, sliver thin and surrounded by a corona of spherical mirrors. Oliver recognized the circular roof of the exam room at Dr. Vincent's office, open to the moonlight, which was being gathered and focused down onto him. He could feel the tension of metal across his body. He was in the mesh cage of the force resonance imager, suspended on his back.

"Hey." Dean leaned over him. "You're back."

Oliver gazed down to see his body glowing bone white. "What happened?"

Dean sighed. "Man, it was crazy. You got hit with the Scourge, and I thought you were a goner. But you just

< 169 >

lay there with sunlight shooting out of your eyes, and your fingertips glowing and stuff, and that was it. Well, plus you were screaming nonstop. I carried you back to your house. Your parents brought you here. They've been cool, letting me check in on you."

"How long?" asked Oliver.

"It's Saturday night," Dean said. "So, two days, about?"

"Two days . . ." Oliver panicked. "What about —"

Dean lowered his voice. "She's all right. I told your parents that we were over on Queen Anne, looking for whoever was using the Scourge. I told them you snuck out because you were so mad about the attacks, and you were frustrated that no one would let you help." Dean smiled a little. "That gave your mom a guilty face for a minute. Nice, right?"

Oliver smiled. "Thanks. So is Emalie at home?"

"At home, and promising not to do the dream enchantment anymore, so she won't be possessed again. Besides, she doesn't need to, now that we know you didn't kill me."

"That's not enough," said Oliver darkly. "My dad and the others will still be looking for her. They'll want revenge for the other slayings. If they have enough time, they'll find her."

"Ahh," a voice echoed across the metal room. "He's

back." Oliver heard Dr. Vincent's footsteps echoing on the metal floor. More footfalls rushed after him.

"Ollie!" Phlox appeared at his side. She grabbed the cage, looking at him with great relief. "We didn't know when you'd wake —" Her eyes burned turquoise, her face twisted as if she was mad, but Oliver could tell the difference between anger and worry. "You shouldn't have snuck out," she said, her voice thick, "but I shouldn't have been so overprotective, I . . ."

"It's okay, Mom," Oliver murmured, hoping this moment would end as soon as possible.

"His levels are almost normal," Dr. Vincent announced. He adjusted a few knobs on a brass console, glancing at the glass computer monitor nearby. The mirrors shut off and the roof began to rumble closed. The FRI rotated, returning Oliver to an upright position. "We should do a follow-up treatment next week," Dr. Vincent continued. He stepped over to them, holding a long syringe filled with warm orange fluid. "Just one more dose for the lingering infection, and we should be in the clear. When you get home, make sure to drink bleach a couple times a day."

"All right, thank you so much," Phlox said.

Oliver felt the sting of the needle, then Dr. Vincent was unlatching the FRI. The body-shaped mesh pulled away from Oliver's skin and swung open.

He stepped down, but wobbled. Dean caught him by the arm.

"We'll see you in a week, Oliver," Dr. Vincent said.

"All right." Oliver nodded blankly.

The three walked slowly to the elevator door. When they were in the cylindrical car, Phlox said slowly: "Oliver, that crystal shard in your side . . ."

"Yeah," Oliver replied. *Here we go,* he thought. One of the many lies was about to untangle itself from the rest.

"Désirée gave you an amulet of Ephyra, didn't she?"

"Mmm." Oliver almost felt relieved to finally have this out in the open.

"She gave it to you the other day, to protect you from the Scourge."

The other day? Oliver tried not to react. "Uh-huh," he said.

"I told your mom," Dean added quickly, "about how she gave it to us the other afternoon, when we were there. Sorry, Oliver." It was all Oliver could do not to show how impressed he was that Dean had lied to Phlox.

"I — I know you wanted to help stop the Scourge," Phlox said, apparently believing it, "and I know you felt like I was babying you."

Oliver nodded. "Kinda," he said, playing along. This meant that Phlox knew about the amulet without knowing about the vision of his human parents. That was a stroke of luck.

"You still should have told me," Phlox went on. "It's not a good idea to just take what Désirée gives you blindly. She often has her own ideas about what someone needs."

They left Dr. Vincent's office, weaving among the hulking black Gasworks towers in the cold, clear night. The air stung, frost on its edges.

"I thought if I told you our plan," Oliver said slowly, making this up word by word, "about getting the amulet for protection, you'd take it away. And I wasn't going to sneak out until I heard about Randall, and how close Bane had been to"— he paused for effect —"well, I just got so angry, I thought I could do something . . . and I didn't think you'd let me."

They leaped over the high fence around the towers. Oliver was happy to find that his side hurt much less without the amulet in it.

"I know," Phlox said, ruffling Oliver's hair as they made their way across the moonlit grass. "It's — well, you're old enough to know that parents don't always know exactly what to do. Sometimes we take a guess. And you're so different, Oliver, with what you've been through recently, with all your power. . . . Well, anyway, I'm just glad you're okay."

Oliver didn't reply. It would have felt good to hear his

mom say these things if they weren't based on such a tangle of half-truths and lies.

They dropped into the sewers and made their way home. Oliver noticed guards still lurking in the shadows.

"So," Phlox said as they entered the house, "Oliver, you really need to rest, but I've thought hard about this, and decided that your father and I will keep our plans for tonight."

"Plans?" Oliver said as nonchalantly as he could.

"We have a standing invitation," Phlox began, slipping off her coat, "to a Valentine's Day feeding over in Bellevue."

Oliver had completely forgotten about Valentine's Day. He remembered distantly that he'd been invited to a party. But then again, his date had been burned to dust, so maybe that was a problem. He couldn't even imagine wanting to go to Suzyn's party now, never mind actually going.

Phlox was opening the hall closet. "It's a Half-Light event, a feeding at a nightclub." She spoke quickly, almost as if she was nervous. She traded in the long black coat she was wearing for one of thick tan fur, then walked into the crypt. "Anyway, the event was going to be canceled, but there's been an outcry in the community. We can't let the Scourge keep us from going about our existence. Your father's at work, but they're letting him off for the evening. I thought I should stay home with you, but . . . I'm going to try to do better at that." She emerged, pinning tiny golden skull earrings in place. "Just promise me you'll stay home, safe, and rest. You need to heal."

"I will." Oliver nodded emphatically. "Promise. Where's Bane?"

"Oh." Phlox waved her hand. "Him. See if I could get him to come visit you at the doctor's . . . but you know your brother. He and his friends are having their own party. I think they were going to hang out at Randall's and harass kids online for a while, then they had a vampire party of some kind. Anyway, I'm sure we won't see him until dawn." Phlox headed back toward the door, then turned one final time. "There's plenty of food upstairs, snacks and stuff. I picked up some of those gorged Malaysian mosquitoes that you like so much."

"Thanks, Mom," Oliver said.

"Okay, then, your father's meeting me on the way, so I should go. . . ." She gazed at Oliver with serious eyes, her hands fidgeting with her handbag. "Oliver, I mean it. Stay here and rest."

"Got it."

"Okay." Phlox nodded, giving Oliver an earnest, tender look. "See you in the morning." She turned and left.

Oliver just stood there as the door slammed. He waited until Phlox's scent faded, then he turned quickly to Dean. "So, Emalie's?"

Dean nodded. "Let's go."

✻

"Thanks, Dean," Oliver said as they emerged from the sewers. "You totally made it work with my mom. That was amazing."

"Yeah," Dean said with a half-smile. "That was pretty good. Man, it's funny, 'cause I used to be terrible at that kind of stuff when I was alive."

"Yeah, lying is definitely easier when you're dead," Oliver agreed, thinking that he was probably the only vampire or zombie out there who actually had trouble with it.

"She really bought it, though," Dean said proudly.

"Yeah, that was . . . different." Oliver almost didn't trust what had just happened, now that he thought about it. But Phlox did love Valentine's Day, and wasn't she right that she'd been too protective of Oliver? *Not if she knew the whole truth*, he thought. But she didn't.

"So," Dean said, "what exactly are we going to do at Emalie's?"

"Not sure," Oliver said. "I think the first thing we should do is figure out how to get rid of that wraith. It can't hurt us as long as we're aboveground and Emalie doesn't leave her body. Then we have to figure out a way to put the blame for the Scourge on somebody else."

"Frame somebody?" Dean asked. "Cool."

They found Emalie's house completely dark. Dean peered in the porch windows while Oliver checked the basement window.

"Maybe they went out for dinner or something," Dean said hopefully. "I mean, that would be a big step for her dad."

They let themselves into the basement. Dean hopped up on the washing machine. Oliver leaned against the sink. The house was still. Oliver heard a few rats in the nearby wall. It worried him that Emalie wasn't home. She shouldn't have left the house. Then again, if she was with her dad, she would be fairly safe, as long as they were in public places.

"Did you hear something?" Dean asked, his head cocked quizzically.

"Huh?" Oliver listened. He only heard the rats —

And now a slight, wet sound. It was very quiet, well beyond the reach of human ears.

"Is that crying?" Dean whispered.

Oliver listened: There it was again, a slight hitch, and sniffles — it did sound like crying.

Something moved in the darkness. It was hard to make out —

"Um," Dean said, "why is there a vacuum bag floating across the room?"

"Something's here," Oliver said, tensing up.

The bag floated smoothly through space, at waist level, barely visible in the faint light from the narrow window. It stopped abruptly in the corner, by an old bike. Then it flipped over and shook. Dust poured downward, floating gently but not evenly. Some of it was stopping in midair. A form was taking shape in the cloud.

"Is that a g —"

"*Tsss,*" Oliver hissed.

A figure had appeared, drawn in dust, small, kneeling on the floor. A hood and shawl had been pushed back, revealing long, matted hair and a delicate face. The dust had blackened where it had landed on wet tear streaks. As the dust settled on long, rumpled robes, the empty bag fell to the floor.

Oliver wondered for a moment if this was a trap, but he felt fairly sure that it wasn't. The dust figure sniffed. "Hey," Oliver said quietly.

"Hey," she replied. Her voice was mouselike, and scratchy with sadness.

"Are you the wraith?" Oliver asked.

The figure nodded. "Not much of one," she muttered.

"I think you were," Oliver said carefully. "I mean, you almost turned me to dust —"

She rolled her eyes. "Almost," she sighed, and slapped at her legs. Dust dislodged, leaving invisible handprints in her thighs. "I was supposed to slay you."

Oliver looked over at Dean. Dean just shrugged. Oliver turned back to the wraith. "Well, the Scourge should have worked, it's just that . . ." He stopped. It was probably a good idea to keep his guard up. "I mean, it wasn't your fault. . . ."

"Tell that to them."

"What do you mean?"

"I was fired," the wraith replied heavily. "Three strikes and you're out. Back to Spira for me. He'll probably send me back to the Shoals."

Oliver had heard of the Shoals. They were spirit borderlands, empty edges: worlds between worlds, full of nothing. "Who's Spira?"

"He's a Merchynt. A big one. He was my broker. He sold me — said I could do the job. And they said if I did, they'd give me passage, but . . . look at me, I failed."

Oliver figured she meant passage from the Shoals into the higher dimensions, where her spirit would be free. So, the wraith had been hired. . . . "What's your name?" he asked.

The wraith finally looked up. While the dust outlined

her delicate face and her eyelids in gray, her eyes were invisible, empty spaces. "Jenette," she said. She seemed younger than Oliver and Dean, but it may have just been her slight build and her light voice.

"Hi, Jenette, I'm —"

"I know you," she interrupted. "Oliver and Dean. Emalie adores you both."

"Um," Oliver began, feeling a flush of nerves, "she said —"

"Where is she?" Dean asked, doing better than Oliver at getting down to business.

Jenette sighed. "Oh. They took her."

"Who?" Oliver asked.

"The same ones who hired and fired me. They never told me their names. And my contract said 'no questions.'" Jenette looked up sheepishly. "I'm really sorry about trying to slay you. It was nothing personal."

"Sure." Oliver nodded, his mind racing. Whoever was behind this must have known that there was a rift between Oliver and Emalie, which also meant that they had been watching them.

"So where is she now?" Dean asked.

"I don't even know," Jenette muttered. "They just cast me out and left me here. Now I can't help you, either. I'll roam forever," she said sadly.

Oliver shared a look with Dean. "Now what?" Dean asked. Oliver was about to answer, when something caught his eye from the small window. Feet, walking by silently.

"Someone's out there," Oliver whispered.

The back door creaked open. A white flashlight beam swept through the basement. "Is anyone in there?" a gruff voice called.

Oliver nodded at Dean, who slid off the washing machine and started squeezing himself between it and a stack of boxes. Jenette shook herself violently, disappearing as the dust scattered. Oliver moved to the wall by the sink and spectralized just as a uniformed police officer crept into the space. His large flashlight arced about. He reached up to the radio by his shoulder and keyed it to life. "Basement looks empty, sir."

"Copy that," a voice replied. "Join the detail upstairs."

The officer slowly left, his flashlight sweeping through Oliver, then into the dark corners of the room. Moments later, his boots ascended the stairs to the first floor.

"That was close —" Dean began.

"*Tss!*"

Oliver just caught the faintest scent, then the lightest footfall — there was someone else down here. He could smell a human man, but barely, almost as if this person knew how to conceal a scent.

The man appeared in the darkroom. He had short brown hair and wore a dress shirt and pants beneath a long gray raincoat, his badge on his belt. He didn't have a flashlight or a gun. Instead, he held a stake.

A radio crackled. He pulled it from his jacket pocket. "Bedrooms are clean, Detective Pederson," an officer reported.

"Check for a crawl space, attic, anything," Detective Pederson instructed. He dropped the radio back into his pocket. "All right," he said softly to the seemingly empty room. "They're all upstairs, Oliver. Now come out."

Oliver didn't move, instead fading back farther into the concrete wall.

"Look," Pederson continued quietly, "there's an alert out for Emalie Watkins. Police are searching all over town. Her father is at the station. I'm just about to report that she hasn't returned to her house, and then I'm sending this detail on to a park where she's been seen hanging out lately. All the officers are going to leave, but then I'm going to stay behind, and if you want to know where she really is, then you'll come out and meet me at my car."

Oliver remained still.

"I hope you make the right choice," Detective Pederson finished. He slowly backed out of the room. Footsteps echoed loudly upstairs as police gave up their stealth. Soon the house was quiet again, and the detective slipped out.

CHAPTER 13

Staesys

Oliver reappeared. Dean slid out from behind the boxes. "Well?"

"Why would a cop be offering help to a vampire?" Oliver wondered aloud.

"He's working with the people who hired me," Jenette said softly from somewhere nearby.

"So it's a trap," said Dean.

"Yeah." Oliver nodded and started toward the door. "Let's go."

"Wait, what?" Dean grabbed his shoulder. "Does the word *trap* mean something different in vampire?"

Oliver wanted to slap Dean's hand off, and maybe throw him against the washing machine for good measure. Here was fearful Dean again, and now was not the time. "It means: That's where Emalie is. They're after me. If getting me makes her safe, then fine." Oliver was hoping that it wouldn't go that way exactly, but if it was dust for him and Emalie would be all right . . .

"Well — but can't we get help?" Dean wondered.

"From who?"

"I don't know, I just . . ." Dean looked into the darkness. "Well, what do you think?"

"I think it's dangerous," Jenette said quietly, "but they are just humans. I could help you."

"How?"

A shadow of Jenette swirled close to them. "They'll try to use the Scourge on you again."

"And this time it will work," said Oliver.

"Another reason why this is a bad idea," Dean moaned.

"Not if you let them," Jenette continued.

"What's that supposed to mean?" asked Oliver.

"If you spectralize right when they hit you," Jenette explained, "I can pull you out, and we can get rid of the Scourge."

"Pull me out, you mean out of this world? That's impossible."

"Well, I can't pull you out forever, but I can pull you into the Shoals for long enough that you can get rid of the Scourge. We can send it off into another world."

Oliver understood what he was hearing. When he spectralized, he was pushing himself along the parallel forces of other worlds, like they were balance beams that he was walking out on. Jenette could pull him farther than he could get on his own. In the Borderlands,

< 184 >

Oliver would exist as energy and could untangle himself from the Scourge. "That could work," he mused, "but how do I know this isn't your next try at killing me?"

Oliver heard a slight laugh in the dark. "You don't," Jenette replied.

He knew it was dangerous. *Maybe I could get my parents, even my brother, anyone. Tell them about Emalie. Maybe if I beg, they'll let her live as long as I never see her again or something.* But that sounded just as risky as what they were about to do. "Okay. Let's go." Oliver started for the door.

Oliver heard Dean sigh and follow behind him. "You coming?" Dean asked Jenette.

"I'll be there," she whispered.

Oliver led the way outside and down to the street. A police car sat idling at the curb, steam curling from its tailpipe. Oliver opened the back door and slid in, followed by Dean.

Detective Pederson glanced back at them. "Everybody in?" he said flatly, and drove off without waiting for an answer.

Oliver felt his nerves sizzling. "How do you know me?" he asked.

"You might not realize it," Detective Pederson began, and Oliver could immediately tell by his condescending tone that this was someone who really disliked vampires. "But you're wanted for murder." Pederson's eyes darted to the mirror again, this time focusing on Dean. "Though I guess that's going to be a little trickier now."

"But you're not arresting us," Oliver countered.

"What good would that do?" Pederson shot back. "An arrest is how a human is treated. A human who is innocent until proven guilty. There's nothing innocent about a demon."

Oliver felt like pointing out that technically, he didn't have a demon. "So then why not just stake me and get it over with?"

"I'd love to," Pederson said coldly. "But I'm not a fool. There's a bigger plan for you."

"As usual," Oliver muttered.

"What was that?" Pederson asked.

"Nothing."

The car continued in silence. Detective Pederson took one turn after another, then pulled to the side of the road. Oliver and Dean looked out the window to see the base of the Space Needle. "Get out," Pederson said simply. "She's up there."

Dean opened the door and stepped out. Oliver followed, slamming the door behind him. Detective Pederson immediately drove off.

"Friendly guy," murmured Dean.

They started across an empty triangle of wet grass. The Space Needle had a narrow, three-legged base that rose up to a large round disc high in the air: a restaurant with windows all around. Fog had rolled in, engulfing the structure halfway up the legs. The restaurant was barely visible, a smudge of light within the mist.

"I came here for dinner once," said Dean, his nerves making him chatty as they approached the gift shop at the base of the Needle. "It was pretty good, except we had to dress up, you know, ties and stuff. It's really nice up there, and —"

"Hello, gentlemen." Oliver halted just in front of the glass double doors that led inside. He turned to find a man sitting on a nearby bench. He was leaning back, one leg up on the other knee, with a computer in his lap. "Glad you could make it." Just by the tone of his voice, Oliver knew they were talking to the one in charge, and yet he didn't quite look it. Instead of being tall, he was shorter. Instead of being muscular, he was overweight. His untucked dress shirt and leather jacket were draped over a wide middle, with baggy jeans. He had frizzy hair, and the blue light from his computer deepened the folds on his face. His pale complexion made Oliver wonder for a moment if he was a vampire, but his scent clearly said otherwise, not to mention his appearance. A vampire adult would never look so unkempt. He stood up, dropped his computer in a shoulder bag, and walked over, hands in his pockets. "I'm Braiden Lang. Nice of you both to come."

Oliver and Dean just stood there.

Braiden shrugged. "Well then, let's get to it, shall we?"

Oliver was just about to reply when he got a better look at Braiden's eyes and realized that his appearance was a trick. This may have been his normal appearance, but the way his eyes darted keenly back and forth revealed that he was capable of, or at least thought he was capable of, very dangerous things.

Oliver and Dean followed Braiden through the doors and across an elaborate gift shop. The lights were off. They reached an elevator and found a black-clad man standing guard beside it, his foot keeping the doors open. They stepped inside. The guard followed. The doors slid closed and the elevator rose up the outside of the Needle.

Windows looked out on Seattle Center's neon world of amusements. Distantly, Oliver heard teens screaming on the roller coaster and at the arcade, trying to impress their dates. The ceiling of fog seemed to lower on them, and then they were swallowed by it, and the view out the window became blank.

"It's nice to finally meet you, Oliver," Braiden said, looking straight ahead.

"Who are you people?" Oliver asked.

"We represent the Brotherhood of the Fallen. We have

protected the Nexia Gate for over two millennia. So you can guess why we've been trying so hard to slay you."

Oliver just shrugged.

"And do you know why we wouldn't want you to open it?"

"No idea," Oliver mumbled. "But you're probably going to tell me."

The elevator smoothed to a stop.

"Nah," said Braiden. Oliver was actually disappointed. He didn't know much about the Gate, but why would humans care about it? How did they even know about it? He was pretty sure it had nothing to do with them.

The elevator doors slid open, revealing the plush, circular restaurant. Its entire outer wall was composed of large windows. The center of the restaurant stayed still, but the ring of floor beneath the dining tables spun slowly, so that customers could see the entire view as they ate. Braiden's associate nudged Oliver and Dean out of the car. Oliver was immediately overwhelmed by a noxious odor, but he couldn't begin to accept what he was smelling just yet. . . . He looked ahead and saw that every table in the restaurant was full.

"What's with the people?' Dean whispered to Oliver.

None of the diners were moving. It was as if they were frozen in time, paused in mid-conversation, midsip, mid-bite. One man was even on his knee, holding out an engagement ring to a woman who was throwing her hands over her mouth in surprise. Meanwhile, the restaurant rotated slowly.

"They're in Staesys," Oliver replied, now seeing the long lengths of red tubing that had been carefully attached to the neck of each frozen human. There were two tubes attached to the back of each neck. They ran straight upward, to hooks that hung from wires stretched across the room. The tubes then dropped down and separated. One tube reached the ground and ran out of sight under the table. The other ended at the tabletop, where it was hooked into a contraption that looked like a water faucet made of brass. There was one faucet for each diner at the table, and there were wineglasses placed beside the faucets.

Oliver knew about the process of Staesys, but since he wasn't old enough to attend such events, he'd never actually seen it. Staesys was a powerful ritual, only done for high-profile events, when a certain amount of elegance was preferred. The entire restaurant had been affected with a transdimensional force called *languessence*. Vampires had imposed the time scale of another world onto all the living things in this room — in this case, from a higher world with slower-moving time. This put the humans into a state of suspended animation.

Once the humans were frozen, the vampire bartenders who catered such events would hook each person up to the tubes. One tube drained the blood to a faucet, where a vampire guest could simply fill their wineglass. The other tube replaced the missing blood with an artificial plasma called sanguinase that would speed the process of blood-making in the humans' bone marrow, so that they would never know what they had lost. Since it was Valentine's Day, the caterers had probably spiked the drinks of these humans with extra-romantic essences beforehand, so that their blood was brimming with passion.

Oliver could tell from the pale complexion of the diners that they had been put in Staesys a while ago, and they had already been fed on, but it was still early. . . . So where were the bartenders? Where were the vampire guests in their formal wear, and the vampire string quartet playing the passionate middle movements of the *Melancholia*? An event of this magnitude would have been held for the senior board of Half-Light, the elders of the Central Council, the barons who owned the magmalight refineries beneath the ocean. . . . Where was everyone?

"Guh," Dean said, looking frustratedly at his feet.

Oliver looked down to see Dean shaking his foot free of something. Now, finally, Oliver accepted the scent that was positively tearing his nostrils apart. . . .

The silver and black ash piles were everywhere.

In the instant that he allowed himself to look, Oliver saw at least thirty dotting the plush carpet, but there had to be more. All the vampires involved in the Staesys — all slain by the Scourge.

"How could you?" Oliver mumbled.

"How could we what?" Braiden retorted. "Slay a bunch of vampires intent on terrorizing these helpless people? I don't know if you realize this, Oliver, but you and your kind are evil."

Oliver almost let his mouth run to defend himself. He thought about pointing out that what these vampires were doing to humans tonight was no different than what humans did to so many living creatures on the planet all the time. As if a human wouldn't hook a cow up to tubes . . .

But the thought was forgotten, because as Oliver averted his eyes from the floor, he caught sight of a table by the window. Sitting there, alone, was Emalie. And she was hooked up to the tubes, in Staesys.

"Hey!" Dean shouted, spying her as well. "She didn't do anything!"

Oliver just stared. It was horrible. She didn't look like she'd lost any blood yet, but still . . .

"You were about to say something?" Braiden chided.

Oliver swallowed his revulsion. "Big deal," he said defiantly.

< 192 >

"Don't even try it, Oliver," Braiden said. "Don't even try to act like you don't care. If you didn't, you wouldn't be here. You wouldn't even be you, but since you are, I wanted this to be the last thing that you ever saw."

There was commotion beside him. Oliver turned to see two men grabbing Dean by the arms. Oliver backed away, toward the table by the window where Emalie sat. Braiden was flanked by more black-clad figures, one man and one woman who had a long scar across her left cheek. All three had their hands clasped in front of them, ready to use the Scourge.

"Why?" was all Oliver could ask.

"They say," Braiden explained smoothly, "that a rebellion is only as effective as its publicity. Well, there's no more public slaying of your vampire kin than this. All these important vampires slain, but worst of all will be finding the ashes of their prophecy child among them. The vampires need to know that opening the Gate is not an option for them. We've stopped them before. We'll stop them tonight. And we'll stop them again. Good-bye, Oliver."

Three sets of hands began to glow. Behind Dean, another man was drawing a long sword.

"Dean!" Oliver had time to shout, and then shimmering heat overwhelmed him, and his insides began to burn. There was no amulet this time. "*Nnnn,*" Oliver moaned. The burning increased. His eyes were overcome with light. He wanted to claw his skin off to release the heat.

Ready? Jenette whispered in his ear. Oliver couldn't respond. He felt his body coming apart, but he tried to focus and spectralize. *Hang on.* Jenette yanked him backward.

In the room, the light went out, and where Oliver had stood, only smoke remained.

CHAPTER 14

Unraveling

The world faded to a distant gray, like Oliver was viewing it through a dusty window. He could still feel the burning of the Scourge inside him, though. Through the pain, Oliver struggled to concentrate, to hold himself together, while also feeling for the parallels of other worlds — but everything was being consumed by light. He could feel the sunlight devouring him. . . .

Here, Jenette said from nearby. *Take my hand.* Oliver felt her small hand close around his. *Just hang on.* Oliver felt himself being pulled, being moved into the strong currents of forces running off toward other worlds. He felt like he was wading into one rushing stream, then another, each pulling in a different direction. He tried to reach for one and push the Scourge into its current, but it seemed to burn away, turning into steam.

Not that one, Jenette said, then stopped in the current of another parallel. *Here. Now. Push.* Oliver concentrated on the Scourge, the energy, getting himself around it like a ball, trying to get it out of him, but the burning only increased.

It's not going to work, he thought. *It's too late.*

No, it's not. He felt hands pulling, helping him, untangling the energy of the Scourge from him, like a knot was being unraveled. Now, finally, it was leaving him. Oliver saw shades of gray, and the blinding white light was in front of him: a glowing, sparking ball, sliding away into mist. The last burning tendrils of the Scourge slipped from him, leaving wisps of smoke behind. He felt cool, but dry, like a burned ember, its light winking out.

I have to get back, he thought weakly.

Wait, Jenette said soothingly. *I can hold you out here for a little longer.* Oliver's eyes cooled, and he noticed her beside him now. Here, he could see her small face, her big eyes. She had long chestnut hair and was wearing flannel pajamas with tiny smiling frogs on them. Jenette glanced at him and seemed to smile a little nervously. She blew her bangs out of her eyes. *Let them think you're gone.*

Beyond her, Oliver saw a washed-out shoreline of gray sand. Water lapped on the shores. The beach of the Shoals seemed to stretch on forever. *Wow,* he thought.

You act like you haven't seen the Shoals before, said Jenette.

I haven't, Oliver replied. *What do you mean?*

Don't worry about it. Jenette reached up and turned him by the shoulders, and Oliver could see back through the smeared window of his reality. There were the members of the Brotherhood, watching the column of smoke that had been Oliver. They weren't convinced yet. Did they know the finer points of vampire powers? Did they suspect a trick?

Oliver saw that one of Dean's attackers was lying on the floor, an overturned table on top of him. The two humans who had been dining at that table were sitting in place as if the table were still there. A loud commotion of falling objects — it sounded like pots and pans — suggested that maybe Dean was holding his own somewhere in the kitchen of the restaurant. Emalie was still frozen.

"Is he gone?" Oliver heard the scar-faced woman beside Braiden ask.

"Either way, let's get the girl and get out of here." Braiden took a step forward.

Why would they want Emalie? Oliver wondered. *I have to go back,* he thought, pushing forward.

No, you have to wait, Jenette said. *Help is coming.*

Help?

From your father.

My f —

Watch.

Braiden had almost reached Emalie when on all sides, windows began exploding inward. Flashes of animals and wings, then black coats — and Oliver saw Sebastian, Leah, Tyrus, Yasmin, and at least five others leaving behind their occupied owls, crows, and bats and leaping into the restaurant. Beside Sebastian was Bane.

Braiden staggered back. Steel flashed as the Brotherhood drew weapons. Oliver saw swords with ornate blades and wooden handles whittled to sharp points at their bases, and crossbows loaded with thick wooden bolts.

Sebastian and the others stood in a semicircle around the perimeter of the restaurant. At once, they held out their hands, one above the other, and puffs of black smoke appeared, becoming long wooden poles with hand-hammered, curved silver blades at one end. Oliver recognized the weapons as the vampires' version of Japanese *naginata* staffs. Vampires rarely chose to fight a straightforward battle, preferring surprise or to create chaos, but these were weapons of war. Sebastian and his team held the poles perpendicular to the floor and stood motionless as the Brotherhood rushed toward them.

"Tachesssss," Sebastian commanded in a hiss. The vampires simultaneously slammed the poles against the floor with a deafening crack and spun into battle. Blades carved the air and clanged together. The room whirled into chaos.

The Brotherhood swung for the vampires' heads, while the vampires went low, blocking blades with the staffs, sweeping at the Brotherhood's legs. The fighting overturned chairs. Tyrus and a Brotherhood member crashed through a long marble table. There was an explosion of dust as a vampire was slain, a brutal scream as one of the Brotherhood collapsed, clutching his torn chest. All around the battle, the humans in Staesys sat unaware.

I have to get Emalie out of there, Oliver thought to Jenette.

I know, she said, and Oliver was confused because he thought he heard a note of disappointment in her voice.

Thanks, said Oliver, *for your help.*

Jenette didn't reply, but suddenly darted up and kissed him on the cheek. Oliver felt the shock of her cold lips on his skin — and she shoved him back toward the world.

Oliver tumbled forward with a rush, through the gray and into the tumultuous reality he'd been watching. He landed on his knees on the restaurant floor, feeling the sting of broken glass that littered the plush carpeting. He had just looked up, shaking the dizziness from his head, when one of the Brotherhood crumpled to the ground in front of him.

"Heads up, bro!" Bane stood over him, blood by his mouth, scanning the melee. "I should thank you for this. What a rush!" His eyes burned with intensity.

"Dad wanted me to tell you: They've got a zip line on the roof. Get your mongrel and get out of here!" He spun his naginata staff, its blade shaped like a dragon's head, then found a sword to meet it.

Oliver got to his feet. He peered through the blur of action. There was Dean, crawling on all fours under the tables, toward him. "Hey! This is cool!" he shouted. "Violence is a lot less scary when you're already dead!"

Oliver grabbed Dean and yanked him to the floor as a sword flashed where his head had been.

"You know," Oliver replied, "you can still have your head cut off and that will be that."

Dean's smile faltered. "Oh, yeah, forgot about that."

Oliver looked up to see the Brotherhood fighter raising his sword again — something sizzled through the air and popped against the side of the man's head. His eyes rolled back and he collapsed. Oliver looked across the room to see Leah holding a slingshot as she crouched atop a table.

"We need to go up to the roof and get out of here," Oliver said quickly, pulling Dean over to Emalie. She remained seated, staring straight ahead with glassy eyes. Oliver moved behind her chair. He placed his hand on the back of her neck with the tubes between his fingers. He grasped the first one and pulled slowly. A long, hollow needle slid out of Emalie's neck, leaving a small bead of blood behind. He pulled the second needle out as well.

"What now?" Dean asked as Oliver pulled her from her chair.

"The Staesys should be broken if we get her out of this room."

Dean looked across the restaurant toward the elevator. "How are we going to do that?" Sebastian and Tyrus were battling with Braiden and the scar-faced woman right by the doors. Sebastian ducked beneath Braiden's thrashing sword, then sliced him across the knee. Braiden howled but blocked the next blow.

"I don't have a demon — we'd be no match for them," Oliver said disappointedly. He glanced around. "Here," he said, picking up Emalie and throwing her over his shoulder. He turned, grabbed a chair, and hurled it through the nearest window. It exploded outward in a rain of glass.

Oliver hopped up onto the edge of a table, for a moment teetering. Looking up, he saw that there was a ledge jutting out above the restaurant windows. Oliver was going to have to leap out and grab its edge. It was only about ten feet out, but also hundreds of feet above the ground, a fall that Emalie would not survive.

"Oliver —" Dean warned.

There was a scream and the clashing of metal from behind him. Something slapped at Oliver's feet. He looked down to see a crossbow bolt embedded in the table.

"Never mind!" Dean shouted. "Go!"

Oliver leaped into space. Emalie's weight was more than he'd bargained for, but he grabbed the edge of the ledge and dangled by one hand, the twinkling suggestion of streets far below through the fog.

"Ehh," Emalie mumbled. "Oliver?" she said weakly. Her face was awkwardly upside down by his armpit.

Oliver used his free arm to slide her back over his shoulder, until her head was upright, her chin on his shoulder. "Hey, Emalie," he said, trying not to sound like they were hanging hundreds of feet above the ground.

"Hey."

"Can you wrap your arms around my neck?" Oliver asked innocently.

"Mmm, sure," Emalie murmured, and did so. "Why am I doing this?"

"It'll just be for a sec," Oliver assured her. "Hold on as tight as you can."

"'Kay."

Oliver swung his other arm up and hauled them onto the ledge. It was made of slats of metal, and there were many spaces for a foot to slip through. Oliver stood, balancing precariously. In front of them was the observation deck that was situated above the restaurant.

Oliver vaulted over this, to the roof. He lowered Emalie until her feet found the sloping metal. She moved beside him, still leaning unsteadily, an arm across his shoulders.

There was a giant array of lightning rods and radio towers at the center of the roof. Oliver saw a thick wire attached to this, slipping out into the fog.

"No problem," Dean grunted. Oliver turned to find him laboring up onto the roof. "Already dead, so nobody lend a hand or anything."

Sirens wailed from below. Oliver saw the lights of police cars dancing through the fog from all directions.

"Oliver!" Oliver turned to see Braiden and the scar-faced woman crossing the roof toward the zip line. Braiden was leaning on one leg, the other bent awkwardly, his knee bloody. The woman began attaching a set of handles to the wire. She ran forward and leaped off the roof, sliding away to safety. Braiden now reached up and flipped his own set of handles over the zip line, balancing precariously on his twisted leg.

"You're a coward!" Oliver suddenly shouted, feeling a new hatred boil for his would-be slayer. He fought the urge to run forward, eyes blazing, as he felt Emalie wobble beside him.

"No, actually I'm a strategist!" He grabbed the handles and prepared to slide away. "Which reminds me," he shouted, "I wanted to tell you about your human parents!"

There was a crash from somewhere on the other side of the roof, a door banging open, and the clashing of weapons.

Oliver couldn't help but stare at Braiden, caught wondering what he was about to say. Braiden smiled. "They're alive!" he shouted, then leaped off the edge of the Needle, disappearing into the fog.

Oliver stared after him, unable to think. Alive? What did he mean? How could they —

"Hey." He glanced over to see Emalie staring at him seriously. "Don't listen to him," she said, trying to shake her head firmly. "We'll figure it out later."

"Okay," Oliver replied blankly, knowing she was right, but inside, it was like a flash had gone off in his mind, erasing everything else. There was no way that was possible. No way. His human parents had been killed. The newspaper had even said so. He'd seen it. . . .

"We should get out of here," Dean added.

Oliver tried to push the thoughts into a dark corner for a while. He started toward the zip line, helping Emalie along, as police car doors slammed below.

"Oliver."

Oliver looked over to find Sebastian on the roof, his long black coat whipping in the wind. A member of the Brotherhood lay at his feet. Oliver saw his eyes dart to

Emalie on his shoulder and watched his face turn blank with what might have been shock, or disbelief, or disappointment, or maybe all three. There was nothing to do, other than just stand there. Oliver wasn't going to put down Emalie — so he didn't.

"Get going," Sebastian said blankly, like he was looking at something he would never understand. "Now." Then he held out his arm, and a crow landed on it. Sebastian dissolved into black smoke that wrapped around the bird and disappeared as the bird flew off.

Oliver stared blankly at the space where his father had been.

"Oliver . . ." Emalie's voice sounded like it was far away. "Let's get out of here."

He shook it off as best he could and led the way to the zip line. He pulled the sleeves of his sweatshirt over his hands and grabbed the wire. "Okay, ready?" he asked. Emalie put her arms around his neck again. Dean grabbed the wire with his sleeves as well. Oliver rushed forward and leaped off the side.

There was a moment of weightlessness, a second of falling, and then the line caught tight, and they sailed down off the Space Needle, over Seattle Center, over the shimmering rides, over the giant fountain — low enough that their feet just kicked the arcing water — and tumbled onto the grass in a dark corner between two buildings.

CHAPTER 15

The Things Said and Unsaid

Oliver lay there for a moment, the Space Needle glowing distantly in the fog. He heard Dean getting to his feet. Offering Emalie a hand. *How could my parents be alive?* he wondered. Emalie's and Dean's faces appeared above him.

"You okay?" Dean asked.

"Yeah," Oliver replied, not knowing if he meant it or not.

They crossed the lawn back to the fountain, and collapsed onto its wall. Behind them was a wide concrete bowl. Inside, a half-sphere of silver metal was shooting columns of water in every direction to the sound of cheery pop music. The water was bathed in pink lights. Groups of kids sat around the edge of the fountain, and some were running around inside, making a game of avoiding the falling water.

"Dude, he was lying," Dean said, stretching out on his back along the wall.

Oliver sat with his elbows on his knees. "Yeah," he agreed, but he didn't believe it. "Maybe."

"We can find out," Emalie said. "Oliver, don't worry."

"Okay." Oliver watched the water and the kids. "I guess we should get you home," he said to Emalie. Of course the idea of home reminded him of that look on Sebastian's face moments ago. Sebastian had seen Oliver with Emalie. All the lies about prodigies would be undone. He thought about Bane, fighting alongside his dad in the Space Needle — a real vampire, a real son — and what exactly was Oliver?

And then something dawned on him. "Ha," he laughed to himself.

"What?" asked Dean.

Oliver shook his head. "They still knew. . . ." he mumbled.

"Who, the Brotherhood?" asked Emalie.

"No, my parents." He looked at Dean. "She was lying."

"Huh?" mumbled Dean.

"My mom," Oliver said, the pieces coming together. "That whole story she told us about going out for Valentine's Day. . . . They knew if they left me alone, I'd sneak out. Then they could follow me, and I'd lead them to the source of the Scourge." He looked at Dean. "After we left Emalie's, my dad talked to Jenette. She knew they were coming."

"Who?" Emalie asked.

"Oh, your wraith," Dean explained with his best careful tone. "She's really pretty nice. I mean, she was just trying to free her trapped spirit. . . . It's understandable, right?"

"*Mmm*," Emalie grunted. She clearly didn't want to hear about Jenette right now.

"So," Dean continued, "do you think your parents already knew about Emalie and the Brotherhood?"

"I don't know what they knew," Oliver finished, "except they knew they couldn't trust me." Realizing this almost made Oliver feel better. His parents — *my vampire parents* — had seen through his lies again. What were they going to do to him when he got home? "Who cares," he mumbled.

"What?" asked Emalie.

"Nothing." He looked to Emalie. "When the Brotherhood had you, did Braiden say why they didn't want me to open the Gate?"

"No," Emalie replied. "They just grabbed me from the basement, without a word. But I bet we can find out about that, too," she added hopefully.

Oliver nodded, and now it sank in that for the first time since back in December, Emalie was talking about things that they were going to do together. He and Emalie and Dean . . . the thought made him smile —

"Oliver?"

Oliver looked up at the sound of the girl's voice. A group of vampire kids had stopped in front of them. There were unknowing human teens passing in clusters as well, coming from the nearby Vera Project, where an all-ages show must have just ended.

"Um, hey," Oliver said, but Suzyn just stared coldly at him.

"Nocturne?" Theo pushed his way to her side. "What's up, Ollie, we thought you might still come to the p — whoa . . ." His eyes widened, taking in the zombie and human that Oliver was sitting with. "No . . . way . . ."

"That's disgusting," Suzyn said coldly. She stormed off, the group quickly following.

Theo was going on as they left, loud enough for Oliver to hear: "Me? Nah, I never doubted that he was a freak. I was just waiting for the right time to let you all know. . . ."

Oliver just nodded and looked at the ground. He waited, listening as the snickering group walked off. He actually felt even more relieved. There. Now everything was back to normal.

"Don't worry about it." Dean patted Oliver on the back. "Let's get out of here."

Oliver shrugged. "Sure."

"Your dad's probably worried about you," Dean said to Emalie.

"Yeah, we should do that," she agreed, then added out of nowhere, "but I want ice cream."

"Huh?" Oliver replied.

"Ice cream." Emalie smiled. "It's a food."

"Yeah, I know. . . . I — okay, sure," said Oliver. Besides, he was up for anything that delayed him going home.

"You were just frozen in time and you want ice cream?" Dean asked.

Emalie turned and punched him in the shoulder, much harder than she would have if he were alive. "Which means I missed dinner," she replied, defiantly cheery, "and now I'm hungry. So there."

"Dick's has milk shakes," Oliver offered. "Some vampires work there, too, so we can get a discount."

For a moment, Oliver, Emalie, and Dean looked at one another. Oliver wondered if they, too, were considering how weird it was to be treating one another like normal friends, despite all the weirdness surrounding it, and all the worry that the future held. And as they took off into the night, he could only hope they were enjoying it half as much as he was.

✦

Eventually, the night had to end. They headed to Emalie's and found her dad worried sick, which seemed to please Emalie as much as it annoyed her.

Standing in the alley behind the house, before Emalie had gone inside, they'd spent a moment figuring out what would happen.

"Let's meet Friday night to try to locate your master," Emalie suggested.

"Cool," Dean said, the idea making him look away nervously.

"And maybe this week," Emalie continued, "I can look for more info on your parents, I mean — your old parents, Oliver —"

"My real parents," said Oliver.

"And there's got to be information about Nexia out there somewhere," Dean added.

"Yeah, online or something," Emalie agreed.

Oliver felt them both look to him. "Right," he said. He liked making plans, but the truth was, these plans involved him surviving whatever was going to happen when he got home.

"Okay, I should go," said Emalie. "Oliver, just — I'm sorry again, about the Scourge."

Oliver met the gaze from her wide, clear eyes and felt a knot twist inside him, tightening and making him want to run away from her — it felt awkward, and annoying, but he fought the feeling, holding her gaze and saying, "It's good. I mean, it's okay. We're good." As he said it, an unrelated thought popped into his mind, from a few nights ago. Something he could do — something he wanted to do . . . But he said nothing about it right then.

Besides, Dean was already snickering at him. "Dork," he chided.

Oliver smiled.

Emalie headed inside. Oliver and Dean watched for a while to make sure things went okay, and when they did, they both headed home.

Oliver's pace slowed as he walked up the sewer beneath Twilight Lane. The familiar feelings of doubt returned as he entered the basement door — the same old anxiety of unknowing, the same old frustration that things had to be so strange, so wrong — but at least there was also a twinge of comfort because, unlike a few months ago, he didn't feel alone now. He also knew that what was wrong with him, at the very least, wasn't totally his fault.

He wound up the stairs and entered the kitchen. Forks and knives were scraping dinner plates in the dining room. Oliver reached the doorway. Phlox, Sebastian, and Bane were all sitting, eating silently. Now Phlox looked up —

And then looked down at her plate without a word. She grabbed her goblet and took a sip. Oliver felt a stab of worry. He saw that Bane had noticed Phlox's reaction and was now wearing a smile miles wide.

Bane, the favorite son. . . . There were more questions for him. Had he known what would happen when he ignited that orb back in the school gymnasium, on the night of Dean's death? Did he even know that someone else had entered that scene?

"Sit down, Oliver." It was Sebastian, his back still to Oliver.

Oliver slid nervously into his chair. There was a plate in front of him, with a perfect slice of butterscotch meringue pie in a chocolate cookie crust. A goblet stood full beside that. Oliver dared a glance around the table. Bane was still grinning at him. Phlox and Sebastian were looking at their plates, eating intently.

What did this mean? Oliver slowly took a bite, waiting for the explosion, the yelling, but it didn't come. Not on the second bite, not on the third . . .

Phlox put down her fork, then dabbed at her mouth with a cloth napkin. "Do you think they will try again, with the Scourge?" she quietly asked Sebastian.

Sebastian paused, fork in midair. "Now that they've lost their element of surprise, I don't think so. We sent them a message tonight, a bloody one. I think the Brotherhood will bide their time . . . at least for a while." The way Sebastian spoke, it sounded as if he'd heard of the Brotherhood before. "Schools will reopen on Monday, at any rate."

"Man," Bane muttered.

Neither Phlox nor Sebastian responded.

Another silent minute passed. Oliver's gut was doing flips. How could they not be saying anything? Were they mad? Why weren't they yelling at him? Was this a good thing? Oliver finished his pie in huge, nervous bites.

"Do you want any more?" Phlox asked tightly, eyes still on her plate.

"No thanks," Oliver mumbled. He had no idea what to do. Should he just excuse himself from the table? That seemed to be what came next. But how could they act like everything was normal? *Maybe they're okay with everything,* Oliver thought briefly, but how could that be?

At that moment, Oliver felt something snap inside. He couldn't take this anymore. *No, don't say anything!* he thought desperately — but then he did:

"So now what?"

Phlox looked up. She met Sebastian's eyes, then looked back down at her food. "What do you mean, *now what*?" she replied softly.

What *did* he mean? *Just drop it!* he thought wildly, but no, he needed to know what this was going to be. "I mean, now what, with me? I — you guys know about . . . about Em —"

"We're not going to talk about it," Phlox interrupted. She finally looked at him, and her eyes were smoldering. "That's what."

Oliver felt a rush of anger. "What do you mean '*not talk about it*'?"

"I mean not . . . talk . . . about it," Phlox hissed. "And you . . ." She paused and took a sip from her goblet. "You're going to get over it."

"Over what?"

"Over her."

"But —"

"That's enough," Sebastian said sternly. "Go get ready for bed."

Oliver couldn't believe it. This was their solution? To not talk about it? He left the table and stormed downstairs, trying to figure out what had just happened.

Later, lying sleepless in his coffin, the thoughts clicked together in his head: *It just means that they don't have a solution. They don't know what to do.* So where did that leave things? *It leaves things stuck right where they are,* he thought reluctantly. Not one place or another. And maybe that wasn't so bad, for now.

Get over her.

Oliver almost laughed. Yeah, right.

❁

After breakfast the next evening, Oliver asked: "Can I go down to Harvey's?"

"Why?" Phlox countered. She was dicing the legs off of a pile of frozen cockroaches on the stone counter. Her chopping seemed to grow louder.

"To get a sorbet," he said simply.

Silence again. "All right." Phlox nodded. "Fine."

"Thanks." Oliver grabbed his sweatshirt before anything more could be said. It seemed that the rules were the same as they had always been. Everything was apparently fine, until someone figured out what to do next.

Well, Oliver knew what he was going to do next. He set out into the night, going two places, neither of which were Harvey's.

✦

When Oliver arrived at the second of his two destinations, he placed a package wrapped in deep purple paper, tied in a crimson bow, on a cement landing. He knocked lightly on the door in front of him — the knock of a coconspirator — then flipped up into the air. He landed on the wall and scrambled quickly to the peak of the roof. Then he flipped over, feet to the overhang of the roof, and hung, inverted like a bat, brushing the hair out of his eyes, and watched the basement door.

There was silence. The door creaked open. Emalie's braided head peered out into the night, glancing left and right. Then she looked down and gave a sharp exhale, the kind that could be annoyance or surprise: With Emalie, it was usually both.

She crouched down and picked up the package, tossing it in her hands a few times. She untied the bow, draped it around her neck, and tore at the paper. The sounds of its ripping startled a cat beneath the nearby parked van.

Emalie balled up the paper and stuffed it in her back pocket. She flipped open a cardboard box, pushing aside folds of tissue paper, and when she saw what was inside, she gave a sharp intake of breath: This one was unmistakable.

Oliver couldn't see her face, but he could tell by the way that she held the clunky old camera out in front of her, letting its worn chrome corners play in the street-light, that she must be smiling. And that made Oliver's gut clench and writhe, burning with anxiety, yet this feeling was something just a little bit different than his usual suffering, than anything he'd felt before —

And it was all the difference in the world.

Below, Emalie held her new camera to her eye, the same model as the one she'd broken. Oliver heard the shutter click — heard the quiet ripple as she advanced the roll of film he'd put inside. She turned, clicked again. Then, without so much as a glance upward, she hurried back into the basement, shutting the door quietly behind her.

Oliver stayed there, hanging still. Then he flipped upward, somersaulting and landing on the roof. He raced ahead and leaped into the air, quieter and faster than he'd ever moved before. Wind and rain whipped at his face. There were worries, there were fears, and most of the future seemed confusing, but for now, Oliver was moving forward, roof to roof, and if he could have glimpsed his reflection, he would have seen a surprising grin.

For more of Oliver's complicated life (and death) here's a sneak peek at what comes next.

The Vandenburg Research Station, located at Prydz Bay on the continent of Antarctica, near the magnetic South Pole of the planet, was a lovely place to spend the month of June if you didn't mind the extreme cold or near total darkness.

Professor Darren Stevens was one of those rare people who found the icy desolation of an Antarctic winter peaceful and relaxing. Watching the sun just edging over the rim of the frozen sea gave him a feeling of relief. He was glad to be so far from all the violence and struggles of daily life. Here, all he had to worry about was the stinging wind, the endless ice, and his geologic instruments.

Day after day of the long dark summer, Professor Stevens sat at his computer, his face bathed in blue light from the monitor, holding his coffee mug with the faded words I SAW MERMAIDS AT WEEKI WACHEE SPRINGS barely visible across the white porcelain, and studied the graphs of his ice core samples. The long tubes of ice were striped with tiny layers of dust and dead microscopic creatures trapped in frozen water. Just a few inches told a million years of history: the global warmings and ice ages, the rises and falls of species and civilizations. It made him smirk at the troubles and pain of the people up North in the sunlight. Didn't they know that their entire lives would only add up to a layer of dust thinner than a fingernail?

Studying the ice cores made the professor less anxious for another reason. People were going crazy about the health of the planet these days, but the ice cores proved that there was no need to worry. No matter how human beings mucked up the Earth, in time, it would fix itself. It wasn't like the world was going to end or anything. It would keep on existing and changing, layer by layer. And so the professor could sit here in the cold quiet night without any worry. . . .

❋

Unfortunately for the professor, there were other beings that enjoyed the dark and didn't mind the cold too much. One of them was standing in front of him now.